THE PONY DETECTIVES

Book Six

Stormchaser
and the Silver Mist

by Belinda Rapley

First published in the UK in 2013 by Templar Publishing,

an imprint of The Templar Company Limited,

Deepdene Lodge, Deepdene Avenue, Dorking,

Surrey, RH5 4AT, UK

www.templarco.co.uk

Copyright © 2013 by Belinda Rapley

Cover design by Will Steele

Illustrations by Dave Shephard and Debbie Clark

Cover photo by Megan Duffield

First edition

MIX
Paper from
responsible sources
FSC
www.fsc.org FSC® C020471

ISBN 978-1-84877-668-5

Printed and bound by CPI Group (UK) Ltd, Croydon, CR0 4YY

For Fran, Tim and their expansive collection
of very welcoming animals,
with special mention to Pinto & Dougie

Rosie and Dancer

Mia and Wish

Alice and Scout

Charlie and Phantom

Chapter One

MIA woke with a start. She propped herself up in the darkness. For a moment she couldn't remember where she was. But as her eyes adjusted, Mia saw the outline of her three best friends, fast asleep under mountains of duvets. Then she remembered – she was in Rosie's bedroom at Blackberry Farm.

An icy mist had rolled in suddenly the evening before. It had moved like an incoming tide, forming what looked like great silver lakes over the meadows. By the time the girls had reached the paddocks to bring in their ponies, the ground was no longer visible and the hedges and trees surrounding the paddocks floated eerily, like islands rising from the silvery deep. The spooky mist had been too hazardous to drive through, and Mia's dad hadn't been able to collect the girls from the yard. So Rosie's mum, Mrs Honeycott, had suggested that Mia, Charlie and Alice should sleep over. Mia had leapt at the chance of staying at Blackberry Farm, where the four friends all kept their ponies. They spent every spare second they could at the farm as it was. But staying overnight was even more fun. Mia loved going to sleep knowing that her pony was just outside, safely tucked up in her stable.

They'd spent the evening in front of the glowing fire in Rosie's cosy living room, tack spread out all round them. They had rubbed their tack until the leather was supple and the buckles shone. With only two more weeks left at school before they broke up for the Christmas holiday, the girls had chatted excitedly about what presents they were going to buy for their ponies.

After dinner they'd braved the cold to check on their ponies, then rushed up the creaky old stairs to get changed into Rosie's spare pyjamas. Then, snuggled under duvets, they'd flipped through old copies of *Pony Mad* magazine before finally drifting off to sleep.

Mia swished her silky black hair over one shoulder. She felt uneasy, wondering what had woken her so suddenly. She sat as still as a statue for a second and listened. But all she could hear was Beanie, Rosie's brown and white Jack Russell, snoring loudly as he lay upside down on Rosie's bed. Mia checked her mobile phone, which was lying next to her: 12.57a.m. She stroked Pumpkin, the huge ginger cat that was curled up near her pillow – he was the best hot water bottle in the world.

"Did you hear anything?" Mia whispered. The cat blinked his sleepy amber eyes and his purr started up like a cranky engine. Mia felt the rumbling under her hand. "No? Well, maybe I was dreaming, then."

As she started to feel the pull of sleep again, she thought of her palomino pony, Wish Me Luck. Mia had put an extra rug on her part-arab mare last night, because it was so cold. She smiled, thinking about Wish delicately tugging at her huge haynet, or dozing quietly in her stable.

Mia yawned and shifted on her airbed,

snuggling back down under the duvet. She'd just closed her eyes, and was starting to drift off again when a distant neigh pierced the silence of the night, beyond the window. Mia jumped up, her heart thudding hard in her chest. A chorus of horse cries rang out in response, this time much closer to the cottage. In a flash, Beanie flew off Rosie's bed. Charlie and Alice sprang out of bed at the same time, and rushed over to pull back the curtains.

"Is that *our* ponies making all that noise?" Charlie asked, her voice croaky with sleep.

"It *must* be," Mia frowned, peering out. "There aren't any other ponies around here."

Rosie rolled over, rubbing her eyes. "Err, why is everyone out of bed?" she asked through a yawn, watching Mia yank a pullover over her pyjama top. "Ooh! Is it breakfast time already? I'm sure I've only just got to sleep..."

"Something's upset the ponies," Alice said quietly, as she unlatched the window and swung it open.

"Alice!" Rosie squeaked, burrowing deeper into her thick duvet in protest. "It's freezing!

You're letting in all the icy air!"

Suddenly another distant, frantic neigh echoed through the swirling mist. In an instant Rosie shook herself awake and jumped out of bed, hopping across the dark bedroom to join the others.

Alice peered into the heavy mist. "We can't even see the yard gate from here, let alone our ponies."

"We'd better get down there," Mia said, turning round to grab the jods she'd neatly folded the evening before. The others began to drag their clothes on over their pyjamas.

Just as they were about to bundle out of the room, they heard a loud creak, followed by a slam and a couple of metallic clonks. The girls stopped in their tracks, looks of dread on their faces.

"Did anyone else think that sounded like a horsebox ramp being done up?" Mia asked, her blood running as ice cold as the mist outside.

"Yes," Rosie squeaked. "But why would anyone be closing up a trailer ramp in the middle of the night, in *this* weather?"

"You... you don't think someone's trying to steal our ponies," Alice choked, "do you?"

An engine started up somewhere beyond the farm.

"We need to get out there," Charlie cried. "Quick!"

The four girls sprang into action. They dashed down the stairs, keeping as quiet as they could. Beanie excitedly wove in and out of their feet, almost tripping them up. They yanked on boots, in too much of a rush to think about jackets or scarves, then Rosie fumbled for the back-door key on the shelf. She dropped it in her panic and knocked heads with Alice as they both bent down to grab it. Once the door was unlocked, Charlie flung it open. The freezing mist enveloped them at once.

Rosie turned on the big, powerful torch she'd grabbed from the kitchen. But all it did was illuminate the thick fog, bouncing the light back at them and making it even harder to see. She turned the torch off and they stumbled towards the gate, feeling their way as they went.

"It's closed!" Mia called out, hoping that was

a good sign. They quickly yanked it open, and ran into the yard. Through the dense cloak of mist, they made out their four ponies' heads looking over their stable doors. The girls breathed huge sighs of relief that they were all safely in their boxes. But from the way the ponies were acting, it was obvious that something was seriously wrong somewhere nearby.

Rosie skidded across the frozen yard to Dancer. For once, her cobby strawberry roan mare didn't mob her for treats. She was standing, just like the others, right up against her stable door. Her fluffy ears were alertly pricked as she looked out into the night, picking up sounds the girls couldn't hear.

In the next stable along, Charlie's sleek black thoroughbred Phantom paced his box, then returned to stand by his door. With his head high he towered over Charlie, staring out unblinking, his whole body trembling. Even when Charlie patted the outside of his rugged neck, he didn't seem to notice that she was there. For a second Charlie felt a tingle of nerves. She'd been terrified of Phantom when she first took him on loan, but over the spring and summer the pair had become inseparable, tuned into each other's every thought. Charlie trusted Phantom with her life. But seeing him like this was a jolting reminder of just what an awesome horse he was.

Wish was the most sensible of the four ponies at Blackberry Farm, but she impatiently shoved Mia away with her muzzle, shaking her head and swishing her cream tail irritably. Alice's dappled grey pony, Scout, was just as agitated as Wish. He let out a piercingly loud neigh. Alice covered her ears as her pony's whole body shook. He set off another wild chorus around the yard, and a moment later replies echoed back from somewhere deep within in the sea of silver mist.

"Those neighs don't sound very far off," Charlie said, jogging over to Scout's stable, where Rosie and Mia had already joined Alice. "There must be some loose ponies nearby."

"We'd better try to find them," Rosie said. "They could be hurt."

Alice nodded. She was excited, but at the

same time, worried about what they might find.

Mia held up one hand to signal everyone to listen, and for a moment the girls held their breath. It wasn't long before another round of desperate whinnies filled the night air. Then, in the heavy silence that followed, they heard the distant drumbeat of thundering hooves.

"Over here," Mia grabbed the torch from Rosie and set off quickly to the far corner of the yard.

The others bundled after her. They clambered over the freezing metal gate at the side of the yard, into the sheep field. They jogged as fast as they could, tripping over tufts of grass, only able to see a few meters ahead. The torch beam pointed at the ground in front of them, bobbing as they ran. The sheep bleated anxiously, dodging out of the girls' path as they crossed the field, making for the hedge at the far side.

"I hope we can find our way back in this mist," Alice panted to Rosie, who was starting to slow. The silvery blanket hung heavily around them, dampening their hair and jumpers.

"We're nearly there, come on, you two,"

Charlie called over her shoulder, impatient to see what was beyond the sheep field. They reached the thick hedge which marked the edge of Blackberry Farm. Beyond was a big, rolling, barren piece of land, nothing but scrub and bare patches of earth. Not that the girls could see any of that as they skidded to a halt.

Suddenly hoof beats thundered past, just beyond where they were standing. Alice caught her breath and gripped hold of Rosie's arm in her fright. "They're the other side of the hedge!"

Mia frowned. "But you can't put horses there, it's just common land. It doesn't belong to anyone."

"Well, there weren't any horses here yesterday," Alice added as the ponies galloped past again.

"No," Charlie puffed, "but then I reckon they've only just got here. Them calling out is what set our ponies off and woke us up."

Mia frowned. "So, if it was a trailer or a horsebox that we heard earlier," she puzzled, "the driver wasn't out to *steal* ponies, they must have been dropping them off, instead."

"Seriously?" Rosie questioned. "Who goes

round dropping off ponies in the middle of the night?"

The girls paused for a moment, feeling confused.

"Well, this hedge is too spiky for us to climb through to check on them," Mia said, not wanting to rip her favourite purple hoodie. "We'll have to go to the end of the sheep field, out onto Duck Lane, and get across that way."

With the torch to guide them, they followed the line of the hedge to the end of the field. They climbed over the livestock gate, jumping down the other side onto Duck Lane. They'd ridden past the piece of common land a thousand times before, and the old, drooping five bar gate at the entrance was a familiar sight. It had never been locked, but it normally stood slightly ajar. Now it was pushed shut. Charlie started off in the direction of the gate, a determined look on her face, but Mia grabbed her arm.

"Careful where you step!" Mia urged. "Any clues will be ruined if you stomp all over them."

Mia shook her head at her friend; Charlie should have known how important clues were by now. After all, the four girls were fast becoming a crack detective team, specialising in solving horsey crimes. They'd called themselves the Pony Detectives after they'd reunited a stolen jumping pony with his owner, and the name had stuck. Since then, they'd got to the bottom of five mysteries. And there was Charlie, about to trample all over any possible evidence!

"We need to concentrate," Mia reminded her friend, firmly.

"I'm trying," Charlie said through chattering teeth, "but it's hard when you're half asleep and frozen to death."

The girls crept alongside the frosted verge and carefully slid between half rotten wooden rails that bordered the common land. The mist was still so thick they couldn't see far into the field. But suddenly the hoof beats thundered back in their direction. Alice gulped. If they couldn't see the horses, then she'd bet that the horses couldn't see them, either. And that meant they wouldn't know to stop... until it was too late.

"Quick, back the other side of the fence!"

she squealed. They dived back through, snagging their jumpers on the wood. They turned back round just as two horses burst into the torchlight, the whites of their eyes flashing. The horses, one bay and one appaloosa, skidded to an abrupt halt at the fence. They turned, trotting with their tails high, snorting wildly before disappearing back into the mist.

"They're not wearing any rugs!" Charlie gasped. "They're going to freeze when they finally stop charging about! Who would have put them here without thinking of that?"

Before anyone had a chance to reply, the horses came storming round once more. They emerged out of the mist and slid to a halt near the gate. The bay opened his mouth and let out another desperate neigh, quickly picked up by the appaloosa.

"There's no grass for them in this field," Alice said, looking round anxiously at her friends.

"They've got nothing to drink, either," Rosie pointed out.

"Well, if we do nothing else tonight," Mia said sensibly, "I think we should at least bring them over some hay and a couple of buckets of water."

"The hay might help them settle, too," Charlie said, hopefully, although she doubted much would do that as the pair spooked, spun round and thundered out of sight once more.

The girls followed the footprints they'd left in the frosted sheep field back to the farm. As they reached the gate, they were greeted by thick sweeping beams of torchlights. Mr Honeycott and Rosie's older brother, Will, were calling out for them.

"We're here!" Rosie called back. "What are you both doing up?"

"We couldn't exactly sleep with all the commotion going on out here," Will huffed, as he and Mr Honeycott stepped into view. "That and the fact that my little sister and her friends disappeared off goodness knows where in the middle of the night."

"Exactly," Mr Honeycott said. He sounded stern, but Alice could see he was worried, and she felt bad. Then his face softened. "What was so urgent that you had to rush out right now?"

"Someone's dropped off a couple of horses on that piece of common land," Mia explained, "just beyond the sheep field."

"They've been racing round like crazy," Rosie added.

"So that's what set off your ponies," Mr Honeycott nodded, then checked his watch. "Right, now, time you four were back in bed. We'll have to deal with the horses in the morning."

"But they can't stay out there with no hay or water!" Rosie protested. "It's bad enough that they'll have to spend a whole night in this freezing cold while we're tucked up cosily in bed."

"We were about to take them something now," Charlie explained.

Mr Honeycott hesitated.

"I guess I could use the quad bike to carry some hay over," Will offered.

"And if we help it'll get done quicker..." Rosie suggested, looking hopeful.

Mr Honeycott gave in. "Well, all right then. But you're not going anywhere until you put some warmer clothes on. At this rate you'll all get the flu, and then you'll be in bed for Christmas."

The girls grinned at Will, then dashed inside to grab the nearest jackets, hats, scarves and gloves they could find. Emerging back into the yard, they lugged a bale of hay out of the barn between them while Will started the quad bike. He balanced the bale on the back, while Mr Honeycott filled a five gallon water container and loaded up three empty buckets.

The girls walked urgently back across the field, closely following the red lights of the slow moving quad bike. Mr Honeycott and Will poured out the water while the girls shook out sections of hay just inside the fence. Within seconds the hoof beats sounded once more, growing louder until the two horses trotted briskly into view. They both drank deeply from the buckets, then moved to the hay mounds, tucking in greedily. They lifted their heads, great clumps of hay hanging down from their chomping mouths. They danced around the midnight feast, still unsettled.

"I wonder if we should stay here?" Charlie thought out loud. "What if anything happens to them?"

Mr Honeycott laughed as he shook his head. "No way. They'll still be here in the morning, waiting for you. And until then, bed."

The girls suddenly felt exhausted as they headed back to the cottage, but their minds were still buzzing. They crossed the yard and said goodnight to their ponies, who were finally starting to relax now the mysterious new horses had stopped their frantic neighing. Dancer, Scout and Wish had gone back to tugging at their heavily filled haynets. Phantom was still standing by his door, looking into the distance, but Charlie could see that he wasn't trembling any more.

When the girls got back inside, dumping their frosted coats and hats by the door, they shook tiny icicles from their damp hair. Mrs Honeycott flitted around them, making hot chocolates to take up to bed, even though it was late.

They changed, dried off their hair and snuggled back into their beds, cupping their steaming drinks. The four best friends looked at each other excitedly.

"We'll have to investigate what's happened to those horses first thing tomorrow," Mia said.

"Sounds like a new case for the Pony Detectives," Charlie grinned, taking a gulp of her piping hot drink, hugging her long gangly legs to her chest.

"It's going to be a busy Christmas," Alice yawned, draining her cup. "What with this and the Greenfield's Riding School Christmas show next weekend."

"*And* the Hope Farm charity ride the day before Christmas Eve," Charlie added, nestling into her duvet.

"Don't forget about the Winter Cup," Mia said. The others looked across, and they began to grin infectiously.

"Of course! How could we forget about watching our first ever polo match?" Rosie giggled. "On New Year's Eve, too!"

She glanced across to a shiny red biscuit wrapper that was sitting on her bedside table. It had the Abbey Polo Club emblem printed on the side. She'd picked up the small packet of biscuits from the Abbey café back in September, at the open day held in celebration of the new polo club that had been set up there. The wrapper was the same bright red as the jackets and polo tops that all the staff at the yard wore, and Rosie had kept it as a memento of an amazing day.

The four friends already knew all about the Abbey itself, because it was renowned for its awesome rides. They didn't head over there very often, because it was a fair distance from Blackberry Farm. But it was their number one destination when they wanted a long hack, as they could always fit in a quality gallop even if the ground everywhere else was boggy or frozen solid.

The girls had never had an interest in polo before the Abbey Polo Club was started up. But this new club was different. It was run by a champion polo player called Nick Webb, whose daughter, India, went to the same school as the girls. India was glamorous and had featured in the local newspaper, the *Eastly Daily Press*, as an up and coming young polo star. She'd even lived in Argentina while her dad was there to train. When they returned to England so that India could concentrate on her GCSEs, Nick Webb got a job managing the highly exclusive Perryvale Polo Club. The Perryvale Club was situated right next to the Abbey grounds, so the girls had ridden past its grand entrance a few times. What they could see from the lane looked plush, but it was mainly hidden from view by huge hedges. They did see Mr Perryvale himself now and again too. They'd often had to jump their ponies onto the grass verge to get out of his way as he flashed past them. They always knew it was him, because he rode around in a polished Range Rover, complete with the Perryvale insignia on the side.

While the Perryvale Polo Club had never really caught their imagination, the Pony Detectives had become fascinated by India Webb. It was earwigging as she chatted to her horsey friends on the school bus that had first sparked their interest in the sport. India had spoken about exercising polo ponies at the

Perryvale Polo Club, riding one and leading three more from the saddle. Then, one morning a few months ago, India had leapt onto the school bus, her eyes sparkling. Her dad was taking the plunge and renting the Abbey estate. He was about to open up a rival polo club, right next door to Perryvale!

The Pony Detectives had got swept up in India's enthusiasm and when an open day was held just before they'd started back at school in September, they'd jumped at the chance to get a peek at the inner workings of a polo yard. The girls had enjoyed a group tour around the smartened up stables. They'd even stepped into the main arena. When no one was looking, they'd pretended to be polo players, galloping their imaginary polo ponies up and down the all-weather surface.

During the Open Day, Nick Webb had been promoting the Winter Cup, a big one-day arena tournament. It was held every year, hosted by different teams in the surrounding counties. Perryvale had hosted it before, and had won it when Nick Webb was the team manager.

This year, Nick would be hosting it at the Abbey. Nick had wanted to drum up lots of interest, and get everyone talking about it. It had worked, and the girls couldn't wait to go back on New Year's Eve to watch the tournament.

Rosie had scoffed the biscuits from the Abbey café ages ago, but every time she looked at the little red wrapper, it reminded her of the excitement to come. She leaned across to turn off the bedside lamp. The girls were still smiling sleepily as they settled back down into the darkness. There was already so much horsey stuff to look forward to in the next few weeks, and now, to top it off, the Pony Detectives had a brand new mystery to solve.

Chapter Two

DESPITE their disturbed night, the girls woke early the next morning, eager to check on the new horsey arrivals. Even Rosie didn't bother trying to sneak an extra five minutes in bed, like she usually did. They rushed downstairs in their pyjamas, and ran into the kitchen to look for their clothes, which Mrs Honeycott had promised to hang next to the Aga the night before. It only took a second to see that the damp jumpers were still sitting in a heap on the kitchen table.

"It must have slipped my mind," Mrs Honeycott smiled vaguely, putting Beanie's food into Pumpkin's bowl, and Pumpkin's into Beanie's.

"Oh, it doesn't matter," Mia said, trying to sound like she wouldn't really mind getting frozen. "We'll just put our coats on." She half knew what was coming next, and was trying to avoid it like the plague.

"Oh, no, you can't go out in this weather without wrapping up warmly," Mrs Honeycott tut-tutted, nodding to the window. The mist had disappeared, leaving a vivid blue sky, and a sparkling frost. "Rosie can lend you some jumpers, don't worry."

Rosie beamed at her friends, who rolled their eyes jokingly and followed her back upstairs. Rosie dug out some of her spare jumpers from deep inside her wardrobe. She dished them out over her shoulder. Alice pulled hers on. The red woolly jumper with a Christmas tree on the front hung limply on her small frame. It fell past her fingers and drooped halfway to her knees. She pushed her mousy fringe out of her eyes, hiccupping back a giggle. Charlie's wasn't much better. She yanked the scratchy-necked sweater over her cropped dark-brown hair. It didn't quite reach the wrists of her skinny arms and barely covered the top of her jods. Charlie and Alice glanced at each other and, with a grin, quickly swapped jumpers. Rosie selected the last jumper for Mia. Mia groaned as she took the rainbow-coloured article, complete with frayed wrists and a hole in one elbow. She quickly smoothed down her long hair and applied a swish of lip gloss, but nothing was going to save her style that morning.

"As long as you're warm," Mrs Honeycott said, as the girls bundled back downstairs, "that's all that counts."

"Really?" Mia sighed, unconvinced. But once she'd hidden the jumper under her fleece-lined purple coat and stepped outside, she was grateful for the extra layer.

"I don't care if it's minus a hundred degrees today," Rosie exaggerated, pulling her woolly bobble hat further down over her ears, "now the mist's disappeared, we can ride later."

The friends walked over to the yard gate. They were greeted by soft whickers from their four ponies, who stood bobbing their heads up and down over the stable doors. Great white plumes of breath blew out into the frosty air.

Alice thought for the thousandth time that

Rosie was so lucky to actually live at Blackberry Farm, just a stone's throw from the ponies. Staying the night here was Alice's favourite thing in the world, besides Scout. She saw her pony yawn, showing his neat, even teeth.

"I think Scout's tired after last night's excitement, too," Alice smiled.

Dancer began to kick her stable door impatiently. "And some of them are clearly tired *and* grumpy," Rosie added, as they all ducked into the feed room.

"Well, Dancer's got a point. The quicker we get sorted here," Charlie said, grabbing Phantom's feed bucket and scoop, "the quicker we can check on the new horses!"

The Pony Detectives hurriedly made up their ponies' morning feeds, stirring the chaff and pony nuts, and mixing in handfuls of chopped carrots and broccoli stems. They quickly carried the buckets across the yard, opened the stable doors and dropped the feeds inside. Even though they were all keen to get to the new horses, none of them could rush off without giving their own ponies some fuss. Charlie kept her fussing to a minimum, knowing Phantom didn't like being mollycoddled. She just gently pulled her black horse's ears as he ate, and rubbed the side of his cheek. Wish broke away from her breakfast to share a cuddle with Mia, while Dancer goggled her eyes as Rosie hugged her chunky neck. Alice stroked Scout's velveteen muzzle. He raised his head and she planted a kiss on the very end of his nose, breathing in the smell of his breakfast. She smiled as his long whiskers tickled her face.

While Alice untied the sagging haynet on Scout's stable wall, the others headed over to the barn. They slid open the huge door and bounced over the straw-and-hay-covered floor to the nearest bales. Once they had broken the bales open, the girls grabbed great armfuls of sweet smelling meadow hay and carried it back the stables for their own ponies' nets. Then Charlie and Rosie ran back to the barn. Between them they dragged a whole bale of hay out into the yard, where Charlie quickly cut the orange baler twine and shoved it in her pocket. Once they'd divided the bale up, the Pony

Detectives set off across the crunchy, frosted sheep field, carrying armfuls between them. The sheep trotted behind them, nibbling at the trailing strands. Rosie was lugging a filled bucket, and squealed when the freezing water sloshed down the inside of her welly boot.

"Careful, Rosie!" Mia sighed. "By the time we reach the field there won't be any water left!"

At the end of the field the girls climbed through the fencing onto Duck Lane, keen to get their first glimpse of the two horses.

"They're still here!" Rosie cried. "We weren't dreaming!"

The horses were standing with their heads close to each other in the middle of the bare, patchy field.

"There's not a single trace of the hay we left last night," Charlie pointed out. "They must have been starving."

The girls climbed into the field carefully and dropped the hay in three piles. The horses cantered over, their heads and tails held high. They stopped just short of the girls, and stood for a moment. The bigger of the two horses, the bay, snorted, shaking his head. The frosted appaloosa stood slightly behind his companion, looking past him shyly to the tempting hay. But neither moved. Instead they just looked over, agitated.

"I think they're nervous of us," Mia said quietly. "We'd better come back out so they can get the hay."

The girls retreated through the fence. Instantly, the dark bay approached the furthest of the three piles. The appaloosa followed, not wanting to leave the bigger horse's side, but wary of the girls. As the horses ate, the girls had their first chance to get a proper look at them. The bay was a rich, dark colour with a white star. He was a similar height to Phantom, but much more solid. His mane was short, and a bit stubby and unkempt. The appaloosa was more finely built, with a big white face speckled with chestnut spots. His mane was just like the bay's – a bit spiky and upright where it was so short.

The girls could see each rib on both horses, even through their thick winter coats.

Charlie tutted. "They need feeding up," she said crossly.

"They're not going to get that staying here," Rosie said, looking round at the barren, weed-strewn field.

"They look nicely bred, though," Alice said, squinting against the bright sun. "Maybe the owners will come back to sort them out today?"

"Well, most people round here know that this land is empty, and that the gate's unlocked," Mia said, leaning against a rickety fence post. "And the horses were unloaded in the middle of the night, without rugs, and left with no feed or water. Whoever left them here can't really care about them, so I wouldn't hold your breath for anyone coming back any time soon."

"Do you think they've been dumped then?" Charlie frowned, shifting her feet as she felt them turning to ice blocks on the frozen grass. She couldn't imagine anyone being so mean as to abandon horses in the icy depths of winter, leaving them to fend for themselves on such poor grazing.

Mia nodded. "Looks like it, don't you think?"

The others had to agree. Rosie walked slowly towards the gate. It stood back from Duck Lane, with a broad earthy verge separating it from the tarmac. "There's a wide tyre track here," she said over her shoulder, "and the earth's freshly broken – probably where a trailer back ramp has been lowered and it's sunk into the ground with the weight of the horses walking down it."

"And here's more proof," Alice said, studying the area nearby, "lots of hoof prints, right where the horses must've been backed down the ramp!"

The rest of the Pony Detectives joined her, being careful not to trample over the area near the gate, in case there were any more clues that could help solve the mystery.

Charlie stared at the ground. The start of a case was always exciting because there was something new to investigate, but it was frustrating too. There were never many clues to go on, although, Charlie reminded herself, they had solved cases before that started from next to nothing. But right now, standing in the icy lane, she was stumped over how they were going to find out who dumped the horses.

Then suddenly, something caught her eye and she felt her heart skip a beat. "Look!"

The appaloosa started and jogged in a circle, away from the dark bay. He stood for a second, then dropped his head again. The girls quietly gathered around Charlie, looking at where she was pointing. "Boot prints," she added quietly.

The girls peered closer at the footprints nestled among the many hoof prints.

"But there's something odd here," Alice said, kneeling down to get a closer look. She ran her gloved fingers over one of the prints. "Whoever dropped these horses off hasn't got identical boot prints. Look at this – the left boot print is complete, but the right boot print is missing the heel part. How weird's that?"

Rosie gasped. "Maybe whoever dropped them off has only got half a foot!"

Mia rolled her eyes. Despite the seriousness of the situation, Charlie and Alice couldn't help collapsing into giggles.

"It was just a thought," Rosie said, trying not to smile as Mia gave her a withering look.

Mia took out her phone and took a photo of the trailer tyre marks, the half boot print and both the horses.

"So, what do we do now?" Alice asked. "There's no way we can just leave the horses here to look out for themselves, can we?"

"Well, there's only one spare stable in the yard at the moment." Rosie frowned. "The other one's having its roof mended. We can't take in one horse and not the other."

"I guess we could start by seeing if any of Wish's old rugs might fit them," Mia said, shivering from standing about in the icy cold for so long. "They might be a bit of a tight fit on the bay, but if we loosen off all the straps we could get away with it. And anything's got to be better than standing around in this freezing weather without anything to keep them warm."

"If we can get near enough to put the rugs on, that is," Alice added. "We might need to wait until they know us a bit better."

"We could see what they're like coming over to us later this afternoon if we put more hay out then," Charlie suggested.

"I guess," Mia agreed reluctantly, as they all stood watching the horses eat. She wanted to get them all tucked up right away. "But at least we can get the rugs sorted out, ready."

"Come on, then," Rosie said, turning back towards the sheep field, suddenly on a mission. "If we're going to come back here later *and* ride today, we better get a move on."

"What's the rush?" Alice asked, jogging to catch up.

Rosie checked her watch. "Because, Alice, I'm standing here watching these horses feed with my tummy rumbling. Mum said that she'd do us eggy bread for breakfast this morning and I'm convinced I can smell it from here! Come on!"

Rosie sniffed the air dramatically, and set off, marching across the field and scattering sheep in her path. The others giggled and followed their friend, suddenly realising how hungry they were, too.

Chapter Three

"IT says here that some horses escaped from Mrs Maplethorp's field the night before last," Mr Honeycott said, reading from his copy of the *Eastly Daily Press*, the local newspaper. Everyone was sitting at the large, battered wooden table, polished smooth over time by countless elbows. It was cosily nestled next to the ancient Aga in the farmhouse kitchen. Mrs Honeycott had made a huge stack of eggy bread, which was rapidly reducing in size.

Alice paused mid-mouthful, looking worried. "Isn't that the second time that's happened recently?"

"The *second* time?" Rosie asked, her voice thick with gooey bread. "It sounds like Mrs Maplethorp's being a bit careless, if you ask me."

Charlie grinned and swatted Rosie. "Not the second time that they've escaped from Mrs

Maplethorp's, dopey. Alice means the second time some horses have got loose from their field."

"Exactly," Mia nodded. "Last time the horses escaped from Long Lane Livery. Remember, a week or so ago – when there was that really bad fog?"

Rosie eyes lit up. "Oh yes! That was just an accident, though, wasn't it?"

"Well, that's what everyone thought at the time," Mr Honeycott said, putting the paper down so that the girls could read the article, "but now it's happened a second time, at a different yard, within the space of two weeks, the police are a bit suspicious. They think there might be a pattern developing."

"It *is* a bit of a coincidence," Charlie frowned.

Mia slid the paper nearer and read out loud to the other girls. "It says here that it looks like seven horses and ponies at Mrs Maplethorp's farm escaped after a gate was opened deliberately. Three of the ponies got onto one of the main village roads, causing chaos. The police have asked all horse owners to double check that their gates are securely locked."

"Mrs Maplethorp's the local Pony Club District Commissioner, isn't she?" Charlie asked.

Rosie grimaced. "She's a real old dragon."

Mia carried on reading. "She said that she didn't notice anything odd, but she thinks she heard a powerful motorbike roaring away at some point during the night."

"They heard a motorbike at Long Lane as well," Alice pointed out, leaning over Mia's shoulder to look at the paper, "it says in here."

"Ooh, what if those horses in the field next door belong to Mrs Maplethorp?" Rosie suggested. "They might have been wandering about and someone passing could have shepherded them onto the common land. Maybe whoever was driving that trailer just spotted the loose horses and stopped to save them. They might not have been dumped after all!"

"Maybe," Charlie said doubtfully. "But I can't see Mrs Maplethorp letting her horses get as thin as those ones looked this morning."

"It's worth checking with her, though, just

in case," Mia suggested. "We can ride there this morning."

"It's quite a long way," Mr Honeycott pointed out.

"We'd better leave now then," Rosie said, clearing away her plate. "Otherwise we'll be late for lunch..."

Alice nudged her. "We've only just finished breakfast, I'm stuffed! How can you even think about lunch already?"

"You always have to plan ahead where food's concerned, Alice," Rosie said, deadly serious.

Everyone thanked Mrs Honeycott for breakfast and dragged on their coats, ready to leave. But before they did, Mia asked if she could keep that page of the paper. Mr Honeycott agreed, and Mia carefully tore out the small article, slipping it into her pocket.

ᘉ ᘉ ᘉ ᘉ

Forty five minutes later, the girls were mounted on their ponies and riding along Duck Lane. Everywhere around them looked like it had been dusted with glitter. Huge cobwebs sparkled in the hedges and a robin flitted in and out of the frosted rosehips.

Wish and Phantom both had exercise rugs on to keep their hindquarters warm as they clopped along smartly, side by side. Behind them, Alice sat in Scout's saddle, hardly able to move under all the layers she was wearing. Dancer plodded next to Scout, curling her head towards the grey pony to keep warm. As they rode, the girls speculated about the new horses' backgrounds.

"Well, if those horses aren't Mrs Maplethorp's, it sounds like we might have *two* mysteries on our hands," Charlie said, turning slightly in the saddle so she could see her friends behind her. "The horses dumped on the common land, *and* ponies being let out of their fields."

"We're never going to get a chance to squeeze in any Christmas shopping at this rate," Rosie grinned. "Mind you, I've got Dancer's presents already, and they're the most important ones."

"Excuse me?" Alice joked. "What about your three best friends?"

Rosie giggled as they turned up onto an iron-hard, rutted path beside a ploughed field.

"It's too frozen even to trot," Charlie groaned, as Phantom stepped gingerly over the lumpy ground. Phantom was on his toes, and Charlie knew that he could do with a really good gallop. But instead, they had to stick to a steady plod.

After another half an hour of riding around the edges of ice-tinged fields and along the verges of slippy lanes, they reached a grey flint cottage. Ponies dotted the fields surrounding it, rugged up warmly and grazing on hay piles. But the gate opening onto the lane had heavy-duty padlocks wrapped around both posts. The first field stood empty.

"Mrs Maplethorp's ponies must have been let out of that gate," Mia said.

Suddenly, a woman wrapped in a head scarf and wearing a thick tweed coat that was almost bursting at the buttons strode out from behind a hedge. She was pushing a wheelbarrow filled with fresh, steaming manure, with a scoop balancing precariously on top. She glared at the girls.

"You're right, this *is* where my ponies were let out," she barked, her pale-blue eyes small in her plump face. "Why, do you know anything about it?"

Mia moved Wish a step closer, and introduced herself and rest of the Pony Detectives. Mrs Maplethorp dabbed her dripping nose with a huge hanky, nodding for Mia to continue.

"Two horses appeared last night in the field next to Blackberry Farm, where we keep our ponies," Mia explained. "We read about your ponies being let out, and wondered if these two might belong to you?"

Mrs Maplethorp stared at Mia during her speech. As she realised that Mia was being helpful, her grumpy features softened. She shook her head. "Got all mine back a couple of hours after they escaped, thankfully. The news spread like wildfire – I had friends all around here phoning to let me know they'd just seen my ponies race past their cottages. Three of the ponies took longer to catch, managed to get themselves onto the main road in the village. Luckily someone grabbed them and got headcollars on them before they came to any harm. Now then, tell me, what do your two horses look like? If they have escaped from somewhere local I might know them."

Mia showed her the photos on her phone and described them both.

Mrs Maplethorp shook her head. "Can't say I recognise them, sorry. Fran Hope might be able to give you some advice about what to do next."

The girls smiled. "Good idea, we know Fran," Mia replied.

"We could go to Hope Farm now," Alice suggested. Scout craned his neck forward, trying to sniff Mrs Maplethorp's barrow of muck through the gate.

"You're some way from there in this direction," Mrs Maplethorp frowned. "And you've hardly picked a good day to go trekking on these icy lanes, you know."

"Oh, but we could cut through the Abbey grounds," Charlie piped up. "And then we could finally give our ponies a good canter on the paths."

Mrs Maplethorp scoffed, and the hardness returned to her heavily-lined features. "You'll be lucky." The girls looked at each other, surprised. "Haven't you heard? The new owner, Nick Webb, has blocked off all the entrances to the Abbey rides. Horrid man. Did it not long after the stables were rebuilt and he moved his polo ponies in. You can't get to a single one of the old rides now."

"But some of the best rides around here are on the Abbey land!" Charlie gasped indignantly, startling Phantom. He hopped forward straight into a dozing Dancer, who squealed with surprise. "He can't do that!"

"Ah, but he can. They aren't bridleways, you see, and that's the problem," Mrs Maplethorp gazed towards the old ruins of the Abbey, which were just visible before the woods. "The old owner, a major in the Army he was, just used to let everyone ride through the estate land without any problems for years. He used to train Olympic show jumpers from those stables years ago, you know. His son owns the place now, though, he's the one that rented it out to Nick Webb. Nick promised that he'd keep all the rides open when he took over. He wanted his polo yard to be completely different from that other snooty place, the Perryvale Polo Club. But no, he's gone all exclusive now, too. The major would be turning in his grave if he knew. Rides around here are less safe for all my Pony Clubbers. Everyone has to stay on roads and face the traffic."

Mrs Maplethorp pursed her lips, looking seriously unimpressed.

"Not only that," she continued, indignantly, "but one of my Pony Club girls tried to ride through the Abbey the other day and came back crying. She said Nick Webb's new estate manager, Mr Pyke, shot his gun in her direction!"

The Pony Detectives looked at each other, shocked. Archie Pyke, Mr Pyke's son, was at the same school as them, in the year below. He'd only just started that term, and he was really quiet. The loudest thing about him was his hair, which was bright red. His older brother, Billy, who was one of the Abbey's top team riders, was just as quiet as Archie. The girls had heard all about him from listening to India on the bus. They couldn't imagine Mr Pyke being so different from both his sons, and so scary.

"My Pony Clubber was convinced Mr Pyke was trying to scare her off the land," Mrs Maplethorp tutted, disapprovingly. "Luckily, she had an experienced, sensible old pony who didn't spook. But it's disgraceful, if you ask me – I certainly won't be supporting Nick Webb's opening tournament, the Winter Cup, on New Year's Eve. And I'm encouraging everyone I know to boycott it too. This man needs to be taught a lesson. I hope I can count on you four to support me, now you know about the rides?"

Mrs Maplethorp gave the girls a formidable stare.

"There's a petition in the village shop to get the rides reopened," she concluded, before striding off with her wheelbarrow, towards the next pile of droppings. "I'd suggest you all sign it!"

With that she disappeared from view, huffing and puffing to herself.

"I was really looking forward to the Winter

Cup," Alice whispered as they turned in the direction of Hope Farm. Their ponies were glad to be moving again, and stepped out purposefully.

"Me too," Rosie said quietly, "but we don't *have* to obey Mrs Maplethorp, do we? I'm still going, no matter what she says."

"Maybe her Pony Clubber just caught Mr Pyke on a bad day," Mia shrugged. There was no way she was going to miss out on all the glamour and thrill of her very first polo match.

"And I bet we can still find a way into the Abbey grounds," Charlie said defiantly. "Mrs Maplethorp and her riders just don't know where to look."

The girls grinned at each other, and began to feel their optimism building once more as they rode towards the Abbey ruins. If anything, getting inside the grounds sounded like a challenge. And with the perfect rides that were waiting inside, it was one challenge they were definitely up for.

Chapter Four

THE Pony Detectives finally reached a T-junction, leading onto Abbey Lane. The lane ran in both directions and, in front of them sat a metal sign, tucked into an evergreen bush. To the right it pointed towards the Abbey. Perryvale Polo Club was to the left. The girls turned down the lane in the direction of the Abbey, starting to get excited about what they might see.

The girls' journey on the school bus took them to the site of the new polo club each day, where the bus would stop by the entrance to the estate to pick up India Webb and Archie Pyke. Smart new post and rail fences separated the edge of the lane from the estate. The posts curved inwards, leading up into the pebbly drive.

An all-weather arena had been constructed

alongside the lane, in the same position as the original sand school. Narrow, young hedges had been planted, obscuring the view of the arena from the road, except at the corner by the entrance where the bus stopped each morning. When the windows were steamed up, the four friends would rub patches clear to watch the riders exercising the flashy, silken-coated thoroughbred ponies on the all-weather surface.

Sometimes the bus would be held up as the Abbey riders and grooms led the ponies in from the fields, allowing the girls a longer look. Each day, they had become increasingly obsessed with one particular polo pony, and as they rode along now they hoped to catch a glimpse of him in the arena.

As they neared the Abbey, Phantom pricked his ears and picked up the pace. Charlie sat quietly, her reins still loose. She smiled, knowing that it must mean he could hear polo ponies being exercised. They rode up to the estate entrance, and stopped at the one corner where they had a bird's eye view of the ponies practising in the arena under their riders. As long as there was no traffic along the lane, they could stay for a few moments to watch.

The polo ponies' legs were heavily protected, with bandages beneath tough leather boots. The bridles had a double noseband, and a cheekpiece made of rope, which threaded through the bit and connected to the lower of two reins. One pony was a pale chestnut without any markings. They recognised his rider, India, at once, her blonde hair flowing from underneath her helmet. The other pony was a bright bay. A white blaze stretched out over both his eyes at the top of his head, and covered his muzzle at the bottom. He moved like a cantankerous bull around the large arena.

"Stormchaser!" Alice breathed as she, Mia and Rosie caught up with Charlie. Without saying anything, the four friends stood, captivated. Stormchaser wasn't a handsome horse, he was brutish and heavily built. But something about him was mesmerising. Stormchaser's rider appeared to sit motionless, as his pony turned on a sixpence and wove around the arena in response to feather touches from the saddle. The rider swung the stick over the top of Stormchaser's neck and leant perilously far to the left, attacking the ball from the near side. There was a 'tock' as the polo stick caught the ball broadside, and almost without asking, the pony took chase, as if he understood instinctively that it was his job to pursue it. India's chestnut couldn't match him, a split second slower to start after the ball. The girls held their breath as Stormchaser picked up speed along one long side of the arena.

"He'll never be able to stop," Rosie squeaked, leaning down along Dancer's neck and almost closing her eyes, waiting for a crash into the arena boards.

The rider reached down and the pony seemed to lean in towards the ball. The rider swept the ball sideways. At once, the pony sat back on his haunches and swung to the left effortlessly. Once more the chestnut was slower to respond, overshooting the change of direction.

"Estoni!" India called out to the other rider, cantering her pony more slowly to the far end of the arena after Stormchaser. "We're meant to be on the same team, remember?"

"So keep up, then," Estoni laughed back cheekily as he cantered towards the end wall, with India behind him. Estoni reached the edge of the arena. He looked over his shoulder and knocked the ball behind him, past India, into the middle of the arena. In an instant, Stormchaser had spun round and was giving chase. India pressed the reins against her horse's neck and sat tight as she also spun round. For a few strides the two ponies held their line, and were galloping side by side, necks outstretched. Just as both riders reached down with their sticks, Stormchaser, a ball of fury and taught muscle, leaned into Rumour, using his bulk to shift the other horse. As brave as a lion, Stormchaser was prepared to barge into any opponent, and he held his own line without flinching. At once the pale chestnut baulked sideways. Stormchaser's ears immediately flickered forward.

The girls watched, transfixed, as Estoni leaned out of the saddle. He swung his stick and sent the ball crashing between the goal posts at the far end of the arena. He stood in his stirrups, and looked up at the Pony Detectives. He raised his stick to them, like a salute. They knew from what India had said on the bus that Estoni was the only professional polo player on Nick's team. He was a magical rider to watch. He seemed to melt into Stormchaser's saddle. The Pony Detectives were in total awe of him, and couldn't help giggling and blushing among themselves when he waved over at them.

"You're such a showoff," India puffed, pulling her pony up, although she couldn't keep the grin off her face as she nodded towards the girls.

"Storm is, you mean," Estoni said in his strong Argentinean accent. "That's why he'll win us our very first Winter Cup. With him on our team, no others have a chance."

The girls exchanged an excited look. They didn't care what Mrs Maplethorp said, there was no way they were going to boycott the Winter Cup. They *had* to see Stormchaser in action.

Estoni turned Stormchaser and pulled him up next to India. But the bright bay wouldn't stand still. He scuffled around the chestnut with his short little stride, his head dipped low, his back humped up. Estoni expertly slid from the saddle, bow legged and awkward in his chunky knee boots. If anything, the bay horse was even more temperamental when the rider was off his back. He fly bucked, hauling Estoni into the air as he gripped hold of the reins grimly. As Estoni led the ill-tempered Stormchaser from the arena, avoiding the horse's swirling head, flashing teeth and striking front hooves, India followed, laughing.

"I think I'd rather stick to old Rumour here," she said, waving goodbye to the girls then giving Rumour an affectionate pat. Her voice trailed off as they disappeared towards the stables. "At least that way I'll get to play in the Winter Cup. You'll probably end up black and blue before New Year trying to control that beast!"

The Pony Detectives continued to stare at the empty arena for a second, before Phantom scraped his hoof. His impatience to be moving again brought the girls out of their dream world.

"Stormchaser is seriously awesome," Charlie

sighed. "It'll be worth coming to see the Winter Cup just to watch him compete."

"I wouldn't fancy going anywhere near him, though, would you?" Alice said with a shiver. "He looks half crazy."

At that moment they heard a sharp cry from the stables just beyond the arena. They stood up in their stirrups, and craned their necks to get a glimpse of the yard. Estoni had managed to get Stormchaser into his stable, but the bay was plunging about in there. As he caused havoc, they caught a glimpse of a shock of red hair as Billy Pyke rushed past in Stormchaser and Estoni's direction, followed by a few of the grooms.

"Make that *full* crazy," Rosie smiled.

"Right! While everyone's distracted we can sneak into the Abbey woods!" Charlie whispered. "Come on!"

The others jogged their ponies after Charlie. The girls rode along the lane for a few minutes, leaving the commotion behind them, looking for an opening in the trees. A small cottage stood, almost hidden from view, in a clearing at the start of the woods. Its chimney smoked cosily. Unsure if anyone was in there, the girls rode clear of it. But just after Charlie turned onto a small path, she came across a huge tree trunk blocking the way.

"Maybe there was some truth in what Mrs Maplethorp said after all," Charlie muttered to herself.

"Back out again," she called over her shoulder to Alice. Scout raised his head and took careful backward steps. Phantom followed.

"There's another place a bit further on," Mia pointed out, "we'll just have to dodge through the trees. That'll still lead onto the gallops."

All of the girls were looking forward to a good blast to warm themselves and the ponies up. Alice scrunched her frozen fingers, worried that she wouldn't be able to grip the reins if Scout took off.

They rode on, until they stumbled across the almost-hidden entrance. It wasn't so much a path, more just a gap in the trees for them to slink through. The ponies picked their way carefully through the gap, towards the main woodland path, which ran along the edge of the estate before curving inwards. They'd nearly reached it when a shout suddenly rang out through the quietness of the wood.

"Here! What do you lot think you're up to?"

Alice almost leapt out of her skin, and Phantom plunged forward, his ears back.

"That's Mr Pyke, the estate manager!" Rosie hissed. "Quick, let's get out of here!"

But Rosie confused Dancer as she tried to turn her in a tight circle between the trees. The stubborn mare planted herself with her nose in the air, refusing to budge another step. The others had already turned their ponies and were hastily making their way back to the lane, when Alice realised that Rosie wasn't behind them. She pulled Scout up. Ahead of her, she saw Charlie and Mia do the same.

"Rosie!" Alice squeaked. "Hurry up!"

But it was too late. Mr Pyke had already stormed over the undergrowth toward Rosie and was standing by Dancer's head, blocking her escape route. He was wearing a long green waxed coat, his red hair curled out from under his flat cap and his camouflage trousers mushroomed over the top of his green wellies. He blended in completely with his surroundings. His face was stony, and he had a double barrelled shotgun, cocked open, in the crook of his arm. Behind Mr Pyke stood his son, Archie, looking awkward.

"This is private property!" Mr Pyke spluttered. "There's to be no riding on this land at *any* time. Is that clear?"

"Well, we always used to be able to ride all over this estate," Rosie said, flushed and indignant. She was trying her best to look like she was standing there because she was seriously brave, rather than because Dancer wouldn't budge.

Mr Pyke looked furious. "That was then, this is now. Things have changed. Now shove off, all of you."

"Mr Pyke, where are you?" Another voice suddenly called over. The girls peered through the trees, and saw a man they recognised from the Abbey open day. It was Nick Webb. He was standing, almost hidden, at the edge of the woods. His expression changed as he noticed the girls and their ponies. A deep frown etched itself on his forehead, between his eyes.

"I'm over here," Mr Pyke shouted back clearly, not breaking Rosie's gaze while he spoke. Alice was transfixed by Mr Pyke's left hand, which was resting on his gun. Mrs Maplethorp's words echoed in her head.

"Well, you're needed up by the Monastery Woods. There's been another... *incident*," Nick Webb sounded like he was choosing his words carefully.

Mr Pyke glanced towards Nick, his eyes glinting. "On my way," he replied. But before he left, he briefly turned his attention back to the girls, speaking gruffly and staring at each of them in turn. "Do yourselves a favour – keep off this estate if you know what's good for you. And you can tell all your horsey friends the same, got it?"

With that, Mr Pyke turned on his heel, and half walked, half jogged towards Nick.

"Come on," Mia said shakily, "let's get out of here."

By the time Rosie finally got Dancer going,

Mr Pyke and Nick had almost disappeared from view. She was about to trot after her friends when she noticed Archie. He had hung behind, and was now standing stiffly against a broad tree. Archie had his own pony, a small grey native called Rascal, and the girls occasionally talked to him about riding, on the school bus. Rosie could tell that he wanted to say something. He turned to look into the woods, hesitating until his dad was out of earshot.

"Um, sorry about Dad," Archie said, nervously. "He... he's not normally that grumpy."

"Grumpy?" Rosie frowned. "Stark raving mad, more like."

At that moment, Mr Pyke's voice boomed out again. "Archie!"

"I've got to go," Archie said, looking panicked and lowering his voice. "But you really *can't* ride in here, it's not safe." Then he turned and raced after his dad.

Rosie watched the figure retreat through the trees, feeling a tingle of fear. "Not safe?" she called after him. "Because of your dad, you mean?"

But Archie didn't stop. Rosie sighed, then

rode out to the others, and told them about Archie's strange warning.

"I get the feeling there's something odd going on inside this estate," Mia said, chewing her lip in deep thought as the four girls began to head off with their ponies. "First of all Nick wants everyone to be involved with his new Polo Club, then suddenly he stops any rider going near the place. Now Archie's saying it's not *safe* to ride in here."

"Well, it looks like Mrs Maplethorp's Pony Clubber was right about the paths being out of bounds," Charlie pointed out. "But why would Nick change his mind about allowing riders in so suddenly?"

Alice scratched Scout's withers for a moment, as the Pony Detectives thought in silence.

"Oooh, he could be worried about his polo ponies being let out?" Rosie suggested. "I mean, the police have suspected there's something dodgy behind the horses escaping from their fields recently. He may just be keeping security really tight before the Winter Cup?"

"Maybe," Alice said, uncertainly. "Although

why close it all down? And allowing Mr Pyke to shoot at trespassers is a bit dramatic, don't you think?"

"It's not the best way to promote the Abbey Polo Club," Charlie agreed.

"We'll have to ask Archie what he meant when we see him on the school bus," Mia said. The others nodded, riding along in silence. Knowing that perfect rides were just tantalisingly out of reach made them even more determined to uncover what was going on inside the ancient Abbey grounds.

Chapter Five

THE four ponies puffed to the brow of the hill, their breath escaping in great plumes. They began to pick their way downwards towards the lane below, beyond which nestled Hope Farm, the ramshackle rescue yard that offered a home to every abandoned and unwanted animal in the area. As the girls and their ponies crossed the lane, a loud, urgent whinny from the nearest field greeted them. At the same moment, a small, scruffy bay pony, with a huge bushy forelock, galloped towards the fence and into view.

"Pirate!" Charlie grinned. Pirate was Charlie's old pony. When she'd outgrown him, she'd put him on loan to Neve McCuthers, who lived in the annex at Hope Farm with her grandparents. Charlie had taken ages trying to find the right rider for her mischievous but fun-loving pony. In the end, Pirate and Neve had found each other, because no one else could put up with his antics. Neve was a natural in the saddle, and a really brave rider. She was the only person Charlie trusted to look after Pirate and give him the home he deserved.

As the cheeky bay pony scuffed to an untidy halt in the field next to them, his fluffy forelock almost covered his bright eyes. Charlie leaned down from Phantom's back to ruffle her old pony's neck over the fence. Pirate stood for a second, breathing a greeting as he touched one nostril first to Scout, then to Wish and Dancer. The girls moved off, and he trotted alongside them as they made their way through the wooden gate and up the track to the yard.

They bumped into Neve as she was coming out of the feed room, crunching on a carrot. After they'd climbed out of their saddles and enjoyed a catch up with their friend, Neve jumped on Pirate bareback and rode over to Fran, who was busy dishing out bales of hay in one of the far fields. Fran finished up and then walked briskly back to the yard, surrounded by her pack of faithful dogs. She crushed each of the girls in a bear hug. Then Mia gave her an update on the previous night's activities.

Fran shook her head, and sighed heavily. "It sounds like a classic case of abandonment, I'm sorry to say. When irresponsible people don't want their horses any more, or can't afford them, they just dump them on land anywhere they can. No longer their responsibility. These ones are thoroughbreds, you think?"

Charlie nodded. "They look like it. They're nice – a bit flighty, but then that's not surprising for this time of year."

"Well, I suggest you put up twenty-one day notices. That makes it clear to everyone passing that the horses have been abandoned, and gives the owner a chance to claim them."

"What happens if no one comes forward?" Alice asked.

"After twenty-one days, the horses can be rehomed legally," Fran sighed. "I've got a stash of those notices, so I'll give you some before you go. I'll bring over a supply of hay and some basic feed, too. In the meantime I'll ring round and see if I can find out any more information."

The girls couldn't help but feel slightly disappointed that putting up notices was all Fran suggested they do. It didn't involve much detective work. Fran noticed their faces and gave Mia a consoling pat on her shoulder, almost sending her flying.

"One thing I've learned from my time here," Fran explained, "is that you can't always uncover an abandoned horse's background, as much as you four might wish to. All too often the old owners just don't want to be found."

As Fran went inside her cottage to fetch the notices, the Pony Detectives gave each other looks. Without saying a word, they knew they weren't prepared to give up that easily. And something being hard to solve wasn't enough to put them off trying. As Alice and Rosie said goodbye to Neve, and Charlie gave Pirate one last hug, Fran gave the notices to Mia, who tucked them inside her thick, waterproof coat.

"Will we see you all on the Christmas Charity Ride?" Fran asked as she helped check girths. She held each saddle's stirrup while the

Pony Detectives jumped back onto their ponies.

"Absolutely," Rosie grinned. Then her eyes popped wide as she remembered what had happened on their ride to Hope Farm. "Although the ride normally goes through the Abbey, doesn't it? You might have to change your route!"

Rosie quickly filled Fran in on what had happened on their ride.

Fran scowled. "Ah, well, you're not the first to flag the problem up. Neve couldn't get into the grounds, either, a couple of weeks ago. No warning, no discussion with the local riders. Nick Webb just closed off the paths overnight. I was fuming."

The girls looked at each other. They hadn't realised how much of an issue it was becoming for everyone in the area.

"We rely on the funds raised by the charity ride to keep going through the year," Fran continued. "I've left messages for Nick, telling him that, but he keeps avoiding my calls. What makes it worse is that before he moved in, he'd agreed to the ride. He even wanted to spice it up with a few fences for the braver riders. Now this! It's just not on. Lots of people have already started to drop out because of the safety concerns with riding on the roads. Anyway, I haven't given up on getting into the Abbey grounds just yet." Fran's eyes blazed with determination. "I've signed the petition. It's not really my style, but right now, I'm willing to do anything to make the event a success. The owner of Perryvale Polo Club, Mr Perryvale himself, mentioned it to me. Said it was pinned up in the village shop. If Nick realises the strength of public opposition, it might persuade him to reopen the rides. Anyway, I must crack on. See you girls later with that feed."

The Pony Detectives squeezed their ponies' sides to get them moving forward, then they all set off back to Blackberry Farm. They'd been out much longer than they'd planned, without a single canter to warm them up, so by the time they got home they were frozen stiff. Their ponies fell upon their hay as soon as they were led into their stables. Dancer didn't even wait until Rosie had taken her bridle off, and most of the long strands got caught around her bit. Then she refused to let the bit go from her teeth, at the expense of losing the half munched mouthful of hay wound around it. The girls quickly groomed the ponies to get their circulation going. Then they put on their thickest rugs, with cosy fleeces underneath. Charlie even put stable bandages on Phantom's legs, knowing how much he hated being cold.

Fran appeared in her old jeep just as they'd finished. The weak afternoon sun was low in the sky and the temperature was starting to drop even further. A fine mist was drifting in once more. Mia had sorted through her huge collection of rugs and identified a couple she thought might fit the abandoned horses. Fran had brought a selection too, along with hay, some feed and headcollars.

Fran walked quietly into the field with them. The bay approached first, spotting the feed buckets, and even gave a quiet flutter of his nostrils. The appaloosa stayed one step behind, but he poked out his nose, keen to have any meal that was on offer. While they ate hungrily they allowed the girls to pet them, and Fran expertly slipped headcollars on both. Between the five of them, they managed to put quilt under-rugs and thick over-rugs with necks on the two horses, to keep them warm. By the time the girls and Fran had finished, the horses already looked happier. The bay even walked up to them inquisitively, shoving at their pockets to see if anything extra was hidden in them, before turning to the large hay piles.

"You'll have to think about names for them," Fran suggested, looking at the horses fondly. "You can't keep calling them *the bay* and *the appaloosa,* can you?"

"Oh, we did that on the ride back earlier today," Alice smiled, as Mia took Fran's laminated notices from her pocket and began to tie them to the fence posts.

"We thought Cracker for the bay," Charlie told Fran, "because he's quite spirited."

"And Frostie for the appaloosa," Rosie added, "because of his markings."

"Well, I think it's pretty clear that Cracker

and Frostie here have been abandoned," Fran said, as she got back into her jeep, "so I doubt anyone will come forward for them. Because of that, I think it's best we get them over to Hope Farm soon. They can get a once over from the vet and the farrier there. And if anyone does pipe up about them before the notice runs out, all you need to do is point them in my direction, and they can collect them from the Farm."

The girls' faces dropped. Fran noticed, and paused for a moment.

"I know you've grown attached to them, but this fencing isn't safe – it'll either cut them to pieces, or they'll end up escaping," she explained. "And you'll thank me when you've got school, your own ponies *and* the dark evenings to contend with."

"I guess," Rosie sighed, stroking one of Frostie's long, floppy ears.

"And I suppose it'd be easy for someone to let them loose from here," Charlie frowned, remembering the ponies that escaped from Mrs Maplethorp's field and from Long Lane Livery.

"There's no lock on this gate, so they could be targeted next."

"Even more reason to move them sooner rather than later," Fran said, as she buckled in and started up the Jeep's engine. "They're nice horses, it'd be terrible if pranksters let them out and something happened to them."

As Fran bumped off down the road, the girls walked back through the sheep field in the gathering gloom. Charlie checked her watch. "If we hurry, we'll have just enough time to go through the clues we've got for our two mysteries before my dad turns up to collect us. We'll have to be quick, though!"

"*And* we can thaw out," Alice shivered, feeling like even her bones were numb with cold.

They jogged the rest of the way back in the thickening mist and called out to their ponies in their warm stables. Alice half wished they could sit in the kitchen and enjoy the heat of the Aga, but they all agreed they should go to the hay barn, where it was more private. Once they'd slid shut the big door and they had all their torches on, it felt cosy in the barn, and, snuggling down under duvets and blankets, the girls began to think about what clues they had. It didn't take long to realise they didn't have much.

"All we've got so far for Cracker and Frostie's case," Mia said, opening her notebook, "is half a footprint, a tyre track and a time for them being dumped."

"And all we have for the case of the ponies being let loose from their fields," Charlie added, "is the sound of a motorbike when horses' field gates were opened."

"There has to be a connection between the ponies escaping from Long Lane Livery one week, and then from Mrs Maplethorp's fields the next, doesn't there?" Alice said. The others thought about it for a second.

"Well, they're either side of the village," Rosie reasoned, "so they're not near each other. And a different number of ponies were let out each time."

"They're completely different set ups, too," Mia added. "Long Lane's a livery yard, and Mrs Maplethorp's is her own home, with ponies in the paddocks next to her. It doesn't seem like there is a connection, other than the motorbike."

"I bet it's some bored idiot, racing round and letting out the ponies for a laugh," Rosie said with a shake of her head.

"I guess it might be," Alice agreed with a sigh, although she couldn't imagine why anyone would think that letting ponies out and scaring them was fun. "But if Rosie's right, it's going to be pretty impossible to track the culprit down."

Charlie grinned. "Although it might be fun trying." She imagined galloping along the grass verges on Phantom, chasing after some terrified biker until he fell off and gave himself up.

"Then there's the weird stuff going on at the Abbey," Rosie reminded the others. "Everyone's talking about Nick Webb closing off the Abbey rides, when he'd originally said he'd keep them all open. Then Archie warns us not to sneak in because it's not safe."

"But he didn't say *why*," Charlie pointed out.

Alice let out another tiny sigh. They'd never had so many problems to solve at once.

She didn't want to say anything to the others, but it was feeling a tiny bit impossible, especially with so few clues.

Just then they heard a car pull up, scrunching on the gravel behind the hay barn. It tooted, signalling the arrival of Charlie's dad, who was collecting Charlie, Mia and Alice.

The girls jumped up, and slid open the huge barn door. With a promise that they'd all think about the clues before school the next day, the Pony Detectives ventured out into the black, icy evening.

♡ ♡ ♡ ♡

On Monday morning, the four friends only just made it onto the school bus. Alice, Charlie and Mia had reached the yard extra early. Rosie had been waiting for them, and came out of the back door, yawning. They'd opened the yard gate, and sorted out their own ponies – feeding, mucking out, turning out – then they had turned their attention to Cracker and Frostie. They'd broken the ice on the water buckets, scooping out the sheets of ice with their frozen fingers, and had just shaken out the piles of hay, when the school bus had turned the corner of Duck Lane. The girls had grabbed their bags and sprinted from the horses' field to the pick up point. For half a second Rosie had thought the bus was going to sail past them, but to her disappointment it had braked at the last moment. Its engine throbbed loudly until they jumped on, out of breath.

As they plumped down into their seats near the middle of the single decker bus, Charlie looked at Mia, and shook her head. Somehow Mia was the only one who didn't have half a bale of hay stuck to her coat, or her hat. She'd even managed to keep her nails clean and, unlike the others, there was no lingering pony smell about her.

Sophie Pope, one of the girls from their class, was sitting just behind the four of them. She collared them before they'd even caught their breath.

"Are you coming to the show this weekend?" Sophie smiled hopefully. "Mrs Greenfield asked me to remind everyone about it."

Mrs Greenfield ran Greenfield's Riding School, not far from the Abbey. Sophie was one of the helpers. A few months ago she'd started to part-loan one of the Greenfield's school ponies, a pretty skewbald mare called Molly.

"I've got a schedule." Sophie dived into her bag, and pulled out a piece of paper as the bus trundled along, in and out of pockets of low lying mist.

The Pony Detectives turned and knelt on their seats to look at the schedule. "I'm doing the Christmas themed fancy dress class," Sophie grinned, "and some of the gymkhana games. What about you four?"

"I'm doing the fancy dress, too," Rosie beamed, "and the clear round jumping, although I'm not sure if Dancer will appreciate jumping with a Christmas pudding on her back!"

"Er, you can get changed in between," Charlie laughed. "I'm doing the Puissance."

"You're so brave," Sophie gasped, "there's no way you'd catch me and Molly jumping a fence that keeps getting bigger each time you clear it!"

Alice and Mia were both doing the clear

round jumping. They sat chatting about it, and about what time they'd need to be there. Rosie got excited when Sophie told them that there'd be a jacket potato stall, and Mia was thrilled to hear there would also be a stall selling horsey gifts.

As they talked, the Abbey broke into view through the fine mist, and up ahead, Billy Pyke, with his shock of red hair, appeared in the lane. He was riding a polo pony bareback, sitting gracefully on top of the pony's rug, holding onto just a head collar and leadrope. From the pony's back, he was leading three more ponies into the Abbey from one of the estate's winter paddocks on the opposite side of the lane.

The bus hissed to a halt at the corner. The doors opened, and Archie climbed aboard. He waved to Billy, who grinned back.

Archie sank into a seat near the front. The bus paused, its engine rumbling. This was the highlight of the Pony Detectives' school day, and they rubbed patches in the condensation on the windows to see out better. Estoni was in the arena, exercising Stormchaser, who was spinning and rearing. As the girls gasped in horror, Archie turned in his seat.

"It's the bus," he explained. "Storm doesn't like it. Estoni says that if he could, Storm would jump out of the arena and take the bus on, like it's some monster horse. He's madly brave."

"Just mad more like," Sophie said, stiffly, with a shake of her head.

At that moment, India came rushing out from the direction of the stables, her long pale blonde hair bobbing behind her. She flew towards the bus, her tie loose around her neck, yanking on her winter coat and carrying her blazer.

The bus driver moaned, as usual, about India being late. She grinned apologetically as she climbed on board.

"I've told you before," she explained, "I have to ride Rumour before school – she needs to be fit for the Winter Cup!"

The driver muttered something under his breath, and the bus jolted forward. Stormchaser took off along the long side of the arena, kicking out at the wooden boards.

"It must be like trying to sit on a fire-breathing dragon!" Charlie laughed, amazed by the powerful force surging out of the bay horse. Phantom was bad enough, but Stormchaser was about a hundred times worse. Nevertheless, Charlie was transfixed by him. She pressed her face against the window until the bus rounded a corner and Stormchaser disappeared from sight.

"Estoni has to ride him at least twice a day," Archie explained, "just to try to keep him under control."

"He's the most talented polo pony there is, though," India smiled, as she paused in her journey to join the year elevens in the back seats. "He came over from Argentina with a huge reputation. It's just been about finding the key to riding him – no one but Estoni can sit on him. Estoni seems to have the magic touch, though, and he absolutely loves Storm. You should definitely come along to the Winter Cup – that's when you'll see Storm really come alive. There isn't a polo pony out there that can touch him. We're so lucky to have him."

Alice noticed that despite India's confident

words, for a fleeting moment her face looked slightly troubled. But then, just as quickly, the smile returned as she moved on towards the back of the bus and Archie picked up the conversation enthusiastically.

"You get to have a go on some of the quieter polo ponies after the Winter Cup, too," he told them. "It's really good fun!"

"You mean we'll actually be allowed to ride *inside* the Abbey?" Sophie said, slightly sarcastically. She turned to face Archie. "I went on a hack this weekend, from Greenfields. Only your dad made it very clear that we couldn't put one hoof inside the Abbey grounds. He was waving his gun all over the place. So why should *we* support the polo match? I think we should boycott it."

Archie's eyes blazed, and he opened his mouth to retaliate. But Alice saw him lock eyes with India, further up the bus. She was giving him a warning look. Archie turned back round sulkily and put headphones on. The beat of music thumped out seconds later. Any hope the Pony Detectives had of finding out more information from him about the Abbey rides had evaporated.

Sophie wasn't finished, but she continued in a quieter voice. "Mrs Greenfield was furious about what happened on the hack. Everyone is, but they're all doing what they can to get the paths reopened," she explained.

"Like what?" Charlie quizzed her.

"There's a petition, it's up in the village shop," Sophie explained. "You should sign it too. The more people that do, the better."

Alice felt a bit awkward, and turned slightly to see if India had heard. It seemed pretty clear that she had. She was looking down the bus towards Sophie, only half listening to her friends. Her bright smile had faded. Alice swivelled back round quickly, before Sophie noticed her watching.

The bus finally left the countryside behind, and houses and congested streets took over. It slowly wove through the heavy morning traffic before pulling up at the school gates. Everyone piled out, but instead of disappearing into school with her friends like normal,

Alice noticed India make a beeline for Archie. India glanced back once to Sophie, then she walked in through the huge doors, bending close to Archie, deep in conversation.

Chapter Six

As the week passed, the girls got increasingly exhausted. They were getting up extra early to sort out Cracker and Frostie, along with their own ponies, before school.

"Maybe Fran had a point when she said how tired we'd get," Mia yawned as they flumped onto the bus on Friday morning. Even Mia's hair was slightly dishevelled and her school shoes a little bit muddy, for the first time ever. Alice and Charlie had to keep nudging each other in double Maths to stay awake, while Rosie's face nearly dipped into her lunch after she dozed off mid-mouthful.

Archie had sat on his own at the front of the school bus all week, making it impossible for the Pony Detectives to strike up a conversation with him. When Rosie did try, on the Friday, he replied with one-word answers and gave her no chance to ask him about their brief conversation in the woods. The only time he brightened slightly was when Rosie mentioned the Riding School show, which was taking place that Sunday. Archie told her he was going too, on his pony, Rascal.

"See you this Sunday, then," Rosie said, as Archie got off the bus in the gathering gloom on Friday afternoon. Archie smiled awkwardly at the girls, but Sophie blanked him. The Pony Detectives watched through the bus window as he and India walked through the entrance to the Abbey.

Nick Webb and Archie's brother Billy were huddled by the grassy entrance to the floodlit arena, mounted on ponies. Mr Pyke was standing next to them, his gun propped over one arm, and Estoni stood facing them all, talking animatedly. He was holding a saddle, and had mud all down one side of him, including his hat, like he'd been flung off a horse. India must have noticed, because she suddenly broke into a run towards him, her blonde hair flying out behind her.

"I bet that beast, Stormchaser, chucked him off," Sophie quipped.

Alice felt her throat tighten. Her first thought wasn't for Estoni, even though he looked like he'd had a hard fall. It was for Stormchaser, and she hoped that he wasn't hurt. As the bus pulled away, Alice turned her head, watching out of the window for as long as she could. But there was no sign of the bay horse. Alice settled back in her seat and caught up with the conversation. It had turned towards the Greenfield's show, which was now in two days time.

"It's my first one with Molly," Sophie smiled nervously. "I can't wait, but I've got butterflies at the same time!"

"That's still how Alice feels now," Rosie said, nudging Alice good naturedly, "and she's been to loads!"

Alice rolled her eyes, nudging Rosie back.

"I've got lots to do tomorrow," Alice said, "including giving Scout a major groom. He's got brown patches up his neck and face where he lies down overnight. He must lie on his droppings. I'm sure he uses them as a pillow."

"I bet they're nice and warm, though," Sophie giggled.

As the bus neared the Blackberry Farm drop off point, the girls wished Sophie luck with all the preparation. Normal lessons were being put on hold so that Greenfield Riding School could be transformed into a winter grotto, ready for the show. On top of that, Sophie had said she was going to groom Molly until she shone, and attempt to plait her mane.

The Pony Detectives jumped off the bus, with Sophie waving from the window. The lights inside the bus glowed bright yellow in the darkening afternoon. The girls didn't turn down the track to the farm, but carried on walking the short distance along Duck Lane.

As they got nearer to the scruffy patch of common ground they saw Cracker and Frostie's heads poking over the gate. The horses' ears were pricked, looking for them. Cracker, as always, was in front of Frostie, and he whickered a soft welcome. The girls gave them loads of fuss, and the apple cores they'd saved from their lunchboxes. The horses wolfed them down happily, then wandered back to the piles of hay that were left over from that morning.

Alice sighed. "I'm going to really miss them when they go to Fran's next Friday."

Rosie nodded. "Me too. I wish this week could last forever." She paused, and thought about it. "Although, we break up from school on Thursday, so on the other hand, I kind of hope it flies by..."

"Well, at least they'll be nicely settled into their new home for Christmas, anyway," Mia pointed out, rubbing Frostie's forehead with her gloved hand.

"Come on, we'd better get Cracker and Frostie's feeds sorted," Charlie said. As the girls headed through the sheep field to the yard, they heard the horses blowing through their nostrils contentedly.

ᘓ ᘓ ᘓ ᘓ

First thing on Saturday morning, the four girls checked on Frostie and Cracker. Then they went out for a quick hack, after Mr Honeycott warned them that mist was forecast to set in again at lunchtime. They ate a hasty lunch in the hay loft, which was too cold to linger in for long, even with blankets, and once they'd tidied up, they headed to the stables to start getting their ponies ready for the Greenfield's show.

They kept the ponies out of the damp, chill air, and groomed them in their stables, chatting to each other through the slatted top halves of the inner stable walls. As the afternoon wore on, the mist masked out the sun, and soon it felt like they were cocooned in the small square yard, with nothing but a sea of silvery white beyond.

"This weather's so grim," Alice sighed, as she looked out into the gloom. "I wish we could bring Frostie and Cracker in." Then she stood back to inspect Scout. He turned his liquid brown eyes on her, listening to her voice. "I bet you'd like them both."

Scout lifted one front leg, tucking his hoof under and waving it slightly. Alice smiled. "I'll see what I can find." She scrabbled in her pocket and pulled out a mint. Scout bobbed his head up and down. Alice had damped his mane down; it had been lying neatly, but had now sprung back up again. Unconcerned, Scout lipped the mint and crunched noisily.

Alice gave her pony a huge hug, then slipped his rugs back on. They were still warm from his body heat, and she almost wished she could wrap them round herself, too. With one last kiss on the softest part of Scout's muzzle, she went to see how the others were doing.

Alice looked over Phantom's door. "He looks amazing – as ever!" she told Charlie.

Charlie shoved her escaping fringe back under her bobble hat, smudging a dirty streak across her forehead. Alice grinned. Charlie was always scruffy, but she made sure that Phantom, with his sleek black coat, looked immaculate. His skin was so thin that he was really ticklish, especially by his back legs and under his girth, so Charlie had to use the softest body brush for him. His coat glistened like satin under the bright stable light. His mane was exactly the same length all the way down, and his oiled hooves finished off his look of perfection.

His arched neck looked powerful and Charlie still couldn't believe that he was really hers to ride. Phantom was tied up, but still danced at the end of his lead rope until Charlie folded his rugs back over him and he was snugly tucked up once more. He gently nudged her arm.

"You're welcome," Charlie grinned, and she and Alice bobbed their heads over Wish's stable. Mia was putting the finishing touches in place. Her mare stood calmly, her eyes blinking contentedly as she soaked up the attention, loving every second of being pampered by Mia. Mia had a wide selection of brushes, and she used every single one until Wish stood fit for any judge in any show ring.

As Charlie and Alice admired Wish, they could hear grunts and squeals coming from Dancer's stable. They giggled to themselves, as silently as they could, until Rosie came to join them, looking red faced.

"She's tried to squish me with her bottom *three times* now!" Rosie puffed. "All because I wanted to plait her tail. Well, she'll have to go without."

"I wouldn't worry," Charlie smiled, as Mia dropped a kiss on Wish's cheek and let herself out of the stable. "Christmas puddings don't normally have plaits, anyway."

Once the girls were finished they spent the afternoon in the kitchen. They wrote Christmas cards to give out at school, which Pumpkin walked all over with his damp, muddy paws. Then they decorated the stables by trailing little coloured lantern lights under the eaves, and hanging their ponies' stockings on the outside of the stable doors.

Back in the cottage, they helped Rosie put the finishing touches to her fancy dress outfit, which mainly involved shoving lots of stuffing into it. Then they sliced carrots, apples and oranges, and mixed them with chaff, treacle and banana to make two sticky Christmas cakes – one for their ponies, one for Frostie and Cracker. Most of the mix seemed to end up on the table or the floor, where it was gobbled up by an ever watchful Beanie. After a vigorous stir from Charlie, one spoonful even flipped out and thwacked the back of

Mrs Honeycott's oversized artist's overalls. The girls fell into silent hysterics, as Mrs Honeycott looked behind her for a vague moment, then wandered off to her painting studio humming a Christmas carol.

Once the cakes were made, they realised that Cracker and Frostie wouldn't be there on Christmas Day. So they took two big, messy chunks straight out to the far field. The two horses slurped and licked their lips, rummaging around the ground for any spare, dropped morsel. Then they came back and licked the girls' hands for ages, their eyes closing softly. It was a while before the Pony Detectives realised how quickly the light was fading.

"We'd better go," Charlie said, patting the horses. She looked across the dark, misty field.

The horses followed them to the gate. They stood watching – Cracker with his handsome head and Frostie with his speckled face and large eyes – until the girls had disappeared out of sight.

The low lying mist wafted in from the meadows, floating just above the yard floor while the girls rushed round sorting out their own ponies. Once evening stables were finished, the girls waited in Wish's stable for Alice's mum to turn up to give her, Mia and Charlie a lift home.

"We haven't got much further with solving any of our mysteries, have we?" Mia sighed, as she automatically stroked Wish's forelock into a neat shape. She looked at the others, feeling a bit guilty.

"To be fair, we haven't had much time," Charlie pointed out. "Not with the evenings being so dark, and this show to get ready for."

"Not to mention two extra horses to look after," Rosie added.

"Mia's right, though," Alice said, thinking about Cracker and Frostie out in their field without any lock on the gate. "I think that as soon as the show's finished tomorrow, we should take another look at all our cases, to work out what we do next."

"Agreed," Charlie and Rosie said, grinning at each other.

Before long, Alice's mum's car had scrunched

down the drive. After the others had jumped in and driven slowly away, Rosie stood by the gate. She noticed the long, searching fingers of mist twist eerily around the yard. With a shiver, she raced inside the farmhouse kitchen and closed the door firmly behind her.

Chapter
Seven

"WHAT happens if I need the loo?" Rosie asked, starting to panic as they rode along the lanes.

It was Sunday, the day of the Greenfields Riding School Show. The mist had been thick through the night, but luckily they'd woken to a fine, frost-encrusted morning. Rosie was wearing a large, brown, pudding-shaped costume. Around the slightly-too-tight neck, was white felt, shaped like icing. Rosie's hat was covered in green felt, with a red stem springing out at the top. Her arms were poking out of holes in the sides, making it difficult to hold the reins in the right place. Dancer was taking full advantage, wandering about all over the lane, looking for any kind of snack available.

"You'll just have to cross your legs," Charlie giggled, setting Alice off again. Alice had been weak with laughter since the moment Rosie emerged from the farmhouse and got stuck in the doorway. The giggles had got even worse when they heaved Rosie into the saddle and she rolled straight over the other side, landing on her back on the floor, with Dancer gazing round at her quizzically. Rosie had been giggling so hard she couldn't even get up without the others' help.

Alice put her own hysterics partly down to nerves, because she was going to be jumping the biggest clear round class at the show. Anything and everything was making her giggle.

They rode past Cracker and Frostie's field, and both horses whickered to the girls' ponies. The ponies whinnied back.

"I bet they wish they were coming, too," Mia said, looking over her shoulder, feeling bad that they were staying behind, "just for something to do."

"There hasn't been any response to those notices yet," Charlie added. "I don't reckon anyone's going to bother coming forward, do you?"

The others shook their heads, still stunned

by the idea of someone abandoning such quality horses. As they rode along, they wondered out loud who Fran might rehome them to, and whether they'd be kept together or not.

"I hope they will be," Alice sighed, "they're really close. Cracker looks out for Frostie all the time."

"Fran will make sure they're kept together," Rosie said, impatiently. "*Anyway*, back to my original question. Did we come up with a solution about what I do if I need the loo?"

U U U U

The girls rode the long way round to Greenfield's Riding School, unable to cut through the Abbey grounds. As they finally turned onto Turpin Lane, Mia frowned at the chaos that greeted them. Trailers and horseboxes were pulling slowly out of the drive. Dodging in and out of them were lots of riders in smart show clothes, and even more in fancy dress. But instead of riding towards the School, they were riding away from it.

"What's going on?" Mia asked.

The others shrugged, frowning and standing up in their stirrups to see if they could catch a glimpse of the yard. They overheard snippets of conversation.

"It's such a shame," one parent, who was leading a small child on a beautifully groomed white pony, tutted, "Lauren's been looking forward to this for weeks."

"I can't believe we came all this way," said another, "and now we've got to turn straight back round again!"

"Excuse me," Mia said to a boy riding past on a smart chestnut, "do you know what's happened?"

"The show's been cancelled," he said, holding his reins lightly. "Apparently some ponies got loose from here last night and they haven't found all of them yet. They've had to call the whole thing off so they can coordinate the search for them."

The girls looked at each other, dismayed. For half a second they all felt bitter disappointment at not being able to compete in the show, but that swiftly turned to determination.

The boy rode on, but the Pony Detectives had no intention of heading home.

"Well, Alice, you said yesterday that we needed to take another look at our cases and work out what to do next," Charlie said grimly, "and now's our chance. This crime scene must only be a few hours old. I think we need to get in there straightaway."

The others nodded, vigorously. They carried on riding against the tide, heading past the fairy lights on the gate, and the huge, highly decorated Christmas tree sparkling next to it. There was a Father Christmas walking about, talking on his mobile and looking anxious. He'd pulled down his big white beard and the girls recognised him as Mr Greenfield. All the stables were trimmed with red and green tinsel, and Christmas carols were still piping in the background. Two stalls were set up near the outdoor arena, but the jacket potatoes weren't being cooked and the horsey gifts were still inside a small truck.

The girls searched for Sophie, and found

her coming back with some other helpers from one of the bridleways that led from the back of the yard. Her eyes were puffy and her cheeks were flushed red. Sophie looked up when they called her name, but she couldn't manage a smile. When Mia asked her what the latest was, Sophie just looked bewildered.

"Molly's still missing," she said all in one breath, a gulp in her throat. "I've been out looking once already, but there's no sign of her, or Biddy, or Samson. I hate to think what's happened to them..."

Sophie clearly wasn't thinking straight. She had headcollars slung over her shoulder but she didn't look like she knew where she was going next, in the confusion around her.

"Which field did they get loose from?" Charlie asked her. "Was it locked?"

"What? Oh, that field over there, the far corner field," Sophie said, pointing over to it. "And no, it wasn't locked, but it *was* tied with baler twine. The horses have never even tried to get out before, though – I don't understand it."

Alice realised that Sophie must not have

linked what had happened with the other ponies being let loose in the last couple of weeks. It didn't feel like the time to raise it, so Alice just asked for details. "Did Mrs Greenfield see anything? Or hear anything?"

Sophie shook her head and sniffed. The Pony Detectives frowned at each other. Then Mrs Greenfield suddenly called Sophie and she turned towards the stables, where the other helpers were gathered. But before she left, she called back over her shoulder to the girls, "Oh, no, hang on. Mrs Greenfield did say she'd heard something… I think she said a motorbike was revving up like crazy, then it raced off. But that's all."

Charlie's mouth fell open and she looked at the others.

"This *has* to be connected to the other ponies being let out, it can't be a coincidence," Charlie said. "Come on, let's see if there are any clues in the field."

They swung their ponies round and walked them up the path that led to the field. The gate was still standing open. They dismounted to lead their ponies closer, then heard hoof beats behind them. It was Archie, trotting his little grey, Rascal, to catch up with them. Archie's face looked pinched as he slid from the saddle.

"What happened?" Archie asked.

"Some ponies were let out of this field last night," Mia told him. "It's the third lot in just over two weeks."

"It's happened again?" Archie blurted out, then bit his lip. He looked anxious, tugging at the tight shirt collar around his neck. Alice noticed, and exchanged a look with Rosie, who'd noticed too.

"Oh, is Stormchaser okay, by the way?" Charlie asked, remembering seeing Estoni covered in dirt after school on Friday. Archie frowned. "After Estoni's fall, I mean."

"No, he didn't fall off *Storm*, luckily," Archie explained, sounding a bit distracted. "He was riding Thimble. Thimble stumbled on one of the gallops, he... he put his hoof down a bit of a hole and sent Estoni flying. Thimble was going to be Estoni's ride for one of the chukkas in the

Winter Cup. He's twisted his fetlock, though, so he's been ruled out."

"Oooh, nasty," Rosie winced, "although it could've been a lot worse, sounds like they were both pretty lucky."

As the girls began to search the area surrounding the paddock gate, they fell silent. Archie glanced at them, then at the ground, too.

"Um, are you looking for something?" he asked.

Rosie tapped her nose. "Clues," she whispered dramatically.

Charlie expanded on Rosie's explanation. "To see if it gives us an idea about who might have done this."

Alice noticed Archie stiffen slightly, as Mia led Wish a couple of steps closer to the gate, then held up the bits of baler twine that had secured it shut.

"I bet one of the ponies leant on that, and it snapped," Archie jumped in quickly, before the others could speak. "It's not much twine to keep all those ponies in a field, really."

Mia turned the twine over in her fingers.

"But why would they suddenly rush against the fence last night, when they've never done that before?"

"It's more likely this gate was opened deliberately," Alice said. "Just like the others."

"And it sounds like the culprit made a sharp exit afterwards on his motorbike," Rosie shook her head.

Archie dropped his gaze, quietly searching the ground, moving some of the hard earth and grass to the side with his boot. Suddenly he pointed off to his right.

"Is that a glove, hanging on that bush over there?"

The four girls turned, ducking under their ponies' necks to get a clearer look in the direction that Archie was pointing. As Alice turned back to check where Archie meant, she saw him crouch down by Rascal's hoof. His pony turned his head to look at him.

"I can't see anything," Alice frowned. "Where did you mean?"

Archie jerked back up at the sound of Alice's voice, sliding his hand into his jodhpur pocket and looking sheepish.

"Oh, maybe I was mistaken," Archie mumbled. He jumped back into his saddle. Rascal immediately turned, ready to go.

"Anyway, I guess I had better get Rascal back," he said, quickly squeezing Rascal into a brisk walk, and disappearing from sight without a backward glance.

The others were about to carry on their search when they noticed Alice staring after Archie.

"What's up?" Rosie asked.

"I can't be sure," Alice said slowly, "but I *think* that Archie slipped something into his pocket when we were looking the other way. I think he distracted us deliberately…"

"You're joking?" Charlie groaned. "And we missed it?"

Alice nodded, feeling sick that they may have just lost a vital clue.

Mia sighed, then turned her attention back to the baler twine in her hand. "Well, one thing we know for certain," she said, "is that those ponies didn't just push their way out of this field, no matter what Archie thinks. This twine's all frayed, like someone's hacked through it with scissors or a knife or something."

"So that confirms it. Someone's deliberately letting ponies out of their paddocks," Alice said. A shiver went up her spine, especially as they still didn't know the fate of the missing Greenfield's ponies. Anything could have happened to them. Scout dipped his head and nudged her elbow, starting to get bored. Alice rubbed his cold tipped ears and leant against his sturdy neck. She glanced round at Phantom, Wish and Dancer. Their ponies were the girls' best friends in the world. What if someone had let *them* out of the paddock, and *they* were charging about the countryside in a blind panic? Alice's stomach churned at the thought of it, she couldn't understand how anyone could be so mean. The criminal at the centre of this mystery must be completely cold hearted, and deep down, she wanted to steer well clear of anyone so cruel. But with ponies' lives being put at risk, she knew she simply didn't have a choice.

The Pony Detectives left the mayhem of Greenfield's and set out to help search for the missing ponies.

"I can't believe I'm having to do serious investigative work," Rosie puffed, "while I'm dressed up as a Christmas pud."

"I think we should ride back past the Abbey," Mia suggested. "The ponies could well have bolted in that direction. We need to ask if anyone there has seen them this morning."

Charlie gave her a sideways smile. "And I guess we might just bump into Archie while we're there..."

"Well, the thought had crossed my mind," Mia replied. I'd really like to find out what he was so desperate to hide in his pocket."

They trotted their ponies on the uphill lanes, telling any riders hacking to the Greenfield's show what had happened.

"Can we walk again for a second?" Rosie panted. "I think I'm starting to overcook..."

"We're nearly there, anyway," Alice said, as they came back to a walk, turning onto Abbey Lane and seeing the Abbey ruins rise in front of them. Billy Pyke was standing by the entrance, glancing over his shoulder, then staring up the road. The girls had never spoken to him before, but they decided he'd be approachable because of the quiet way they'd seen him handle the polo ponies.

"Hi there," Mia called over. As he looked over at the group, and scowled, Mia started to wonder if they'd got him wrong. "Er – some ponies were let out of their fields last night at Greenfields Riding School—"

Billy started slightly and cut Mia off rudely. "So what's that got to do with me?"

"Oh, nothing," Charlie said, taken aback. "It's just three of them are still missing, and we wondered if you'd seen them, that's all. One of them was a skewbald—"

"I don't know anything about it, all right?" Billy snapped back.

"We were just asking," Rosie said, indignantly. "Don't you care that there might be terrified ponies wandering around here?"

Billy glared at her darkly. He was about to answer when a silver estate car rounded the corner at speed. It skidded to an abrupt halt. Billy forgot the girls in an instant as he leapt up and grabbed at the car door, yanking it open. He jumped in and the girls heard a snatch of his conversation.

"Rumour's up on the grass gallops."

Then the door slammed shut, and the car accelerated away, spitting out gravel from spinning front tyres. It turned into the entrance of the Abbey estate and disappeared inside. Phantom skitted sideways, his head up as Charlie rested one hand on his neck to soothe him.

"Come on," Alice said, slightly taken aback, "if everyone at the Abbey's this rude we're not going to get any help here."

"And I guess this isn't the time to try and sneak in to find Archie, either," Rosie said, looking down at her pudding shaped body.

"Not exactly," Mia agreed.

Charlie shivered. She wanted to keep moving

as Phantom still felt tense beneath the saddle. "We're not going to find the ponies standing about. We might as well keep riding – they could be anywhere round here."

The girls touched their heels to their ponies' sides. They made their way along the lane, until the woods petered out at the boundary of the Abbey estate. At that point, the trees were replaced by tall, dense holly bushes dotted with bright red berries, which the girls couldn't see through.

Mia paused by Perryvale Polo Club's gated entrance, and looked up the long, tarmac drive. Grazing near the gates were horses in smart rugs, chomping on piles of hay in their neatly pooh-picked fields.

"Do you think we should ask here about Molly and the other loose horses?" she asked the others. Mia desperately wanted to have a sneaky look round the glamorous club, but she also genuinely thought it might help find the missing ponies. The others slowed their ponies to a halt, unsure about heading into the vast, private estate. Then they heard a car engine and prepared to move their ponies to the side of the lane, out of the way. But the shiny grey Range Rover, complete with smart royal blue Perryvale Polo Club insignia on its side, stopped beside the girls instead of turning into the drive and its window rolled down smoothly.

"Ah, just who I wanted to see," a large, stocky man with a broad smile and thick black hair leant out of the open window. He puffed on a fat cigar. The Pony Detectives recognised the Range Rover, and the man inside; it was Mr Perryvale himself. The girls shared a quick, surprised look between each other. Mr Perryvale had never spoken to them before, and they didn't know whether to be excited or worried. After all, why would *he* want to see *them*?

Rosie tried to look serious and important, to make up for the fact that she was dressed as a Christmas pudding.

Mr Perryvale smiled even wider, as if sensing their uncertainty and wanting to put them at ease. "You four are local riders, aren't you?" The four girls nodded, feeling wary. "Ah, good. That means you may well be able to help me out.

A couple of my grooms found a few ponies roaming loose on the lanes early this morning. They came from the direction of the Abbey Polo Club, although I notice that no one from there bothered to do anything about them... Anyway, my grooms have taken the loose ponies up to my stables to keep them safe. Don't suppose you know who they belong to, do you?"

"Oh, is one of them a skewbald?" Alice asked, brightening, as she realised that Mr Perryvale actually seemed really friendly and helpful.

"That's it – pretty thing, all plaited up," Mr Perryvale smiled, taking another puff on his cigar.

The girls grinned, pleased by their stroke of luck. "They were let out from Greenfield's Riding School last night." Charlie explained.

Mr Perryvale's smile faded. "Another lot?" he said, in his rich, deep voice. "Tut tut. I heard about that business at the other two places. Sheer luck none of the horses have been injured – not yet, anyway. But, of course, this isn't the first time that horses have been let out of their fields for no apparent reason. There was another incident – oh – some months ago now."

Mr Perryvale let his words linger in the air for a moment.

"Really?" Mia asked, frowning as she and her friends exchanged a questioning look. "We didn't hear a thing about that!"

Mr Perryvale raised one eyebrow. "I thought it was common knowledge," he purred. The girls stood waiting impatiently, wondering if Mr Perryvale was going to carry on. But instead he picked up his mobile phone, holding one hand up for quiet while he dialled a number. Then he spoke to one of his grooms, telling them where the ponies came from.

"Organise the lorry to take those ponies back," he said grandly, "and call Mrs Greenfield to let her know that they're safe and on their way home."

The girls exchanged a quick look, impressed by his generosity. "Now, where was I? Oh yes, that incident a few months back. Young chap was caught in the act."

"So, who was it?" Charlie asked, her heartbeat starting to quicken.

"A young man, on a motorbike," Mr Perryvale said, puffing on his cigar again. The girls looked up sharply. "Thought it would be funny to open a gate and chase the ponies inside the paddock out onto the lanes."

The girls knew that they were all thinking the same thing – it was sounding pretty similar to what had happened at three yards in the last three weeks.

Mr Perryvale continued. "It wasn't widely reported at the time. That was just because I thought I could deal with it myself. Now I wonder if that was a mistake, given what's happened recently."

"What do you mean, you thought you could deal with it yourself?" Rosie asked. She hoped Mr Perryvale would stop talking in riddles and hurry it along a bit. Dancer had just licked the bonnet of the highly polished Range Rover and left a big, grassy smudge. She wanted to escape before Mr Perryvale noticed.

"I tried to smooth it over with everyone concerned, because the young man responsible was working for me at the time, you see,"

Mr Perryvale said dryly. "It was a bad business, very bad. If word had got round that someone from my yard had been letting ponies loose in the village, well, it wouldn't have looked very good for the Perryvale Polo Club. I had no choice but to sack the young fella. His father worked for me, too. I would have kept him on, but he said if his son was going, he'd go too."

Mia frowned, her brain starting to whizz from wondering who it was that let the horses out.

Mr Perryvale took another thoughtful puff of his thick cigar. "Still, he found a new job quickly enough." Mia noticed the large man glance toward the Abbey. "*Some* people aren't so fussy about who they employ, it seems."

Mr Perryvale looked back to the girls, and smiled once more. "Anyway, must dash. Thanks again for your help with identifying the ponies."

"No probl—" Charlie started to say, as Mr Perryvale's window smoothly buzzed upwards. Before she'd even finished the second word, the Range Rover had rolled off up the long drive.

Chapter Eight

THE girls didn't hang around once they got back to the yard. They slipped off their ponies' tack and brought them brimming haynets. Once they'd slung rugs over the ponies, and tucked them up warmly, the girls headed for the farmhouse. In the cosy kitchen, Charlie, Mia and Alice helped haul Rosie out of her fancy dress, then they all raced up the stairs to change from their show outfits back into their usual riding gear. They ran downstairs again, grabbed their packed lunches and the hot chocolate that Mrs Honeycott had quickly whipped up, and headed for the hay barn. As they hungrily scoffed their lunch, they went back over the new information they'd got that morning.

"So, we know that three lots of ponies have been let out," Charlie said, biting into a cheese and onion pasty. "At Long Lane Livery, Mrs

Maplethorp's and now Greenfield Riding School. And each time a motorbike's been heard nearby."

"And now we know that someone who used to work for Mr Perryvale was caught letting out horses from a paddock a few months back," Alice added, wrinkling her nose. "Do you think it's the same person now, back to their old tricks again?"

"Maybe," Rosie agreed, inspecting her turkey and stuffing roll before taking a big bite. "But we still don't know who that person was, so it doesn't exactly move the case forward, does it?"

Mia grabbed her notebook from its hiding place in the barn and between mouthfuls of sandwich, turned to a clean page and wrote three neat headings:

Cracker and Frostie

Ponies Being Set Loose

Abbey Polo Club

"Mr Perryvale may not have told us a name," Mia said, "but did anyone else notice him glance at the Abbey when he mentioned it? I reckon the guilty person works there."

"In that case Mr Perryvale must be right…" Charlie added. "Nick Webb really can't be fussy about who looks after his horses."

"We already know he's not fussy, though, don't we," Alice sighed. "He lets Mr Pyke get away with shooting his gun near horses." She couldn't help feeling disappointed that the Pony Detectives' early excitement about the Abbey Polo Club was disappearing seriously fast.

"Do you think that's why Archie was looking so shifty earlier, by the paddock?" Rosie asked. "Maybe he's got some inside information about who's been letting the ponies out?"

Charlie gasped, and almost fell off the hay bale she was perched on.

"What is it?" Mia asked, a bit miffed Charlie had thought of something before she had.

"Mr Perryvale might not have named the person responsible," Charlie said breathlessly, "but he said it was a young man and his dad…

Archie's brother, Billy, works for the Abbey, and so does his dad, Mr Pyke! It has to be them, doesn't it?"

"Billy's one of the polo riders at the Abbey," Mia added, feeling her heart start to quicken. "So he could have been employed by Mr Perryvale, along with his dad!"

"Totally!" Rosie beamed. "How many other father and son pairs work at the Abbey? I'd bet my lunch that they're the only ones! Oh, hang on – I'll bet my empty wrappers. I've finished most of my lunch already."

"Well, there's only one thing for it," Charlie said, standing up and sounding determined. The others looked at her. "We have to get back into the Abbey. We need to see if there's any evidence there that could pin this on Billy."

"Like what?" Rosie asked dubiously.

"I don't know yet," Charlie said. "But if we can find out where Archie's cottage is, we might be able to sneak in and find out what it was he slipped into his pocket at Greenfields."

"Charlie!" Alice cried. "We can't break into people's houses!"

"All right, maybe not," Charlie agreed, sheepishly. "But we can't just sit around here, either. Let's get our ponies tacked up again and go out. They haven't done much yet today, so they'll be okay. Otherwise we'll have to wait until next weekend because it'll be too dark after school. Come *on!*"

Despite Charlie's enthusiasm, Alice felt her heart flutter slightly. The thought of bumping into Mr Pyke and his gun again made her shudder. But she wasn't about to admit that, and she followed close behind the others as they flew back out to the yard.

The air was growing even chillier, but the girls barely noticed. They quickly slid their ponies' bridles on, and were back on Duck Lane before Dancer had a chance to protest at turning out again.

It wasn't until they were half way to the Abbey that the mist started to snake through their ponies legs. It wrapped itself round the girls like a freezing blanket, only revealing the next few metres in front and behind them.

"What do we do now?" Alice asked

nervously, as the group slowed. She knew that if a car came along, even if it was going slowly, it wouldn't see them until the last second. And to try and stay hidden in the Abbey woods, they'd left off their hi-vis gear. All they could hear was the clop of their ponies' hooves, the noise bouncing off the mist and echoing around them. Scout's step became more unsure and his ears flicked back and forward, like he was checking with Alice if everything was okay.

"Look, there's the turning onto Abbey Lane," Charlie said, finding herself whispering, without knowing why. She could just about make out the metal sign, and knew that the Abbey was to their left. "We're here now, so we might as well carry on. And look on the bright side – this mist will give us the perfect cover for when we get into the woods!"

But Charlie was the only one who was keen to carry through their haphazard plan. Even Mia felt uncertain, now they were about to actually sneak into the Abbey grounds. She knew, though, like the others, that this might be their best chance to get inside and find some clues.

She just wasn't sure now they were actually here *what* they hoped to find. But even if there was just the tiniest chance of uncovering the truth behind the ponies being let loose, it was worth sneaking in for a dig around. If they didn't, it was just a matter of time before a horse got hurt.

"Come on, then," Mia said, gritting her teeth as they turned up the lane. "Let's get this over with."

At the edge of the murky woods the girls dismounted, but the last path they'd tried had already been blocked off. They began to search for another gap big enough to shimmy the ponies through, but had no luck. To Alice's relief, they were about to give up, when a hushed cry came from the front of the group. It was Charlie, who was still at the front.

"Here!" she hissed, as quietly as she could. The others led their ponies over to her, and in a snaking line, they walked into the dank, misty woods.

The ponies' hooves turned from metallic clangs to dull thuds as they stepped from the lane onto the peaty, woodland floor. Charlie had to hold a fractious Phantom with one hand and try to clear a path with the other as her horse tried to charge forward. They slowly made their way in the direction of the little cottage they'd seen previously, hoping it would be Mr Pyke's. Distant but familiar voices soon told them that it was.

"Shh, everyone!" Charlie whispered over her shoulder. "It's just through the trees ahead!"

The four girls could smell tangy wood smoke coming from the cottage chimney. They stayed back with their ponies, standing where they could just see the outline of the cottage, straining to hear what they quickly realised sounded like an argument by the open back door.

"I've told you already, Archie! We can't afford for anything to go wrong here, we *have* to make this place a success, no matter what. And that involves you keeping your mouth shut."

Mia glanced round, and mouthed the words 'Billy' to the others, who all nodded, recognising his voice at once.

They could just make out Billy's silhouette at the doorway to the cottage, with the light behind him. They could see that he was holding out something, but the mist was too heavy to tell what it was. Billy quickly pulled on a jacket and the girls saw Archie follow him out of the cottage. Their school friend looked worried. Billy hopped down the wooden steps and was about to walk away, when he paused and turned back to his brother.

"Listen," he said. "You did the right thing earlier. But don't go and spoil it all by shooting your mouth off. Dad and Nick mustn't hear about this. I'll sort everything out, trust me. All right?"

Archie nodded, sinking against the door frame, as if he wasn't sure what to do next.

With that, Billy strode over to a shed next to the cottage. He slung the doors open and disappeared inside. Archie suddenly seemed to come to life, and rushed after him. He stood anxiously outside the shed.

"You can't go over there now!" he called, his voice anxious and reedy. "It's too misty! Billy, don't!"

A few seconds later they heard an engine

splutter, then burst into life. The girls watched, as Billy emerged on a motorbike. It sounded high-pitched and tinny. The girls exchanged silent looks, their eyes almost popping out of their heads. Phantom pulled back on the reins, scaring himself as he tangled his hooves in the splintering undergrowth. He gave a short, explosive snort. Charlie quickly soothed him, one hand on his high neck, her heart racing as she glanced through the trees to see if her horse had alerted Billy and Archie to their hiding place.

But Billy had his helmet on. He revved the bike and sped towards the Abbey entrance, oblivious to the girls in their hiding place. As the sound of the engine's exhaust faded, Phantom continued to back up, scrunching through the brambles. Alice held her breath as Archie lingered at the doorway. Charlie soothed Phantom, and the other ponies stood stock still. Suddenly the silence was broken as Dancer let out a loud, lingering fart. Rosie's mouth dropped open in horrified surprise. The girls desperately tried to stifle their hysterics, for fear of being discovered. But they needn't have worried; Archie seemed lost in thought. In the next breath he turned back inside the cottage and quietly shut the door behind him.

∪ ∪ ∪ ∪

Even as the girls stood there, the mist began to waft away, slowly revealing more of the estate.

"Well, that confirms it, don't you think? Billy Pyke's got a motorbike, and that's like the last piece of the puzzle," Charlie said, struggling to hold onto an increasingly agitated Phantom. "It has to be him that got sacked from Perryvale Polo Club, and this proves that he *must* be up to his old ways again!"

"I thought he looked guilty earlier when we asked him about Molly and the Greenfield's ponies!" Mia said, triumphantly.

"The question is, why would he do it?" Alice asked. She felt excited about finding out who was behind the mystery, but a tiny part of her couldn't help feeling disappointed, too. Billy might have been grumpy with them, but they'd seen him being nice to the polo horses. "What would make him do something that might end up hurting ponies?"

"I don't know," Rosie said, "but I don't think we should hang around here to try and figure it out, do you?"

"Rosie's got a point," Mia agreed, "the mist might be disappearing but it'll be getting dark soon. Come on. We'll have to try and work it out later."

But with tangled brambles on the ground, not to mention the tightly packed trees, it was difficult to turn round. After a few minutes scrabbling about, the ponies got upset and anxious. The girls decided it would be better to go forwards and find the woodland gallops.

"There must be an open exit we can slip through at the top end of the Abbey land," Charlie said, trying to sound confident.

"What if they're all sealed up, though?" Rosie asked. "We might be trapped." She was still feeling nervous. They hadn't spotted Mr Pyke yet, which meant he could be lurking anywhere with his gun.

"We'll have to risk it," Mia said, her cheeks getting red as she tried to stop a restless Wish from stepping into any brambles that might cut her legs.

Charlie, Mia and Alice sprang back into their saddles, while Rosie struggled to bounce up onto a shifting Dancer. But as soon as they were mounted, their journey through the woods became easier. Rather than having to find paths wide enough for them and their ponies to walk side by side, their ponies could just pick their own way through the dense woodland.

They rode, through pockets of mist, until they joined their favourite Abbey track. The Pony Detectives recognised it at once, even though they would normally reach it from a clearly marked entrance into the woods, straight opposite the stable yard.

The track curved gently uphill, through dense trees on either side. Beyond the trees to their right, the Perryvale estate began. The woodland track was wide enough for two horses to be ridden next to each other, and it was springy under hoof.

The ponies were still on edge, picking up on the girls' mood.

"Is everyone okay for a canter up here?" Charlie asked, as Phantom coiled up like a spring beneath the saddle. Her arms were aching from trying to contain him, and she didn't know how much longer she could hold him. And she couldn't put her finger on why, but now they'd used up their luck not being discovered by Billy and Archie, she wanted to get out of the Abbey as quickly as possible.

The others agreed. As soon as Charlie softened her fingers on the reins, Phantom bounded forward. She heard the rhythmic beat of the other ponies trotting behind her. With barely the slightest shift in her weight, Phantom picked up canter. Charlie took her weight out of the saddle, and balanced over Phantom's withers. Her horse lengthened his stride, his mane flowing as he began to calm beneath Charlie.

Charlie felt herself starting to relax, too. The only thing they had to worry about now was finding a way out at the top of the estate. But she was sure there'd be another gap between trees further along the boundary. She felt herself start to smile, enjoying the thrill of sitting on a horse as powerful as Phantom, when suddenly a shot rang out into the silence, filling the air. It echoed in Charlie's ear as loudly as if it had been fired right next to the path, right at her.

Phantom seemed to pause in the air for a second, stunned, before pinning his ears back and bolting. Charlie grabbed the front of the saddle quickly, trying to stay on top as Phantom flew into a wild, uneven gallop. She knew he was running blind, in a panic that had taken him straight back to instinctive flight. There was no way she could turn Phantom, the path wasn't wide enough, and all the time he was going straight he was picking up speed. She was almost being thrown out of the saddle with each stride, and one foot had slipped through her stirrup iron, making it difficult to balance as they galloped in and out of low lying mist patches.

All Charlie could do was hang on until her horse began to tire, but she knew Phantom, and she knew that moment may take some time to come. Charlie was aware of shrieking behind her, but she didn't dare turn round. She didn't know if the others were still on board, or if any of them had come off. All she could think about was how stupid someone was to fire a gun that close to horses.

The end of the wooded track loomed up ahead, suddenly appearing out of a patch of mist. Charlie had ridden up this path lots of times, and it used to peter out, then lead into a dirt track. But out of the swirling mist in front of her emerged a line of newly planted, tall hedge plants. Charlie closed her eyes, and braced for the impact, but Phantom swerved to the left at the last moment, narrowly avoiding them. Charlie somehow clung on, hanging sideways out of the saddle and losing a stirrup. Then they were careering off again along the edge of a field, following the new hedge.

The icy cold air she was gulping in was burning her chest, and she had no idea where the path was taking her; the mist patches meant she couldn't see far ahead. She pulled on the reins, but Phantom was still in full flight mode, and there was little she could do.

Suddenly Phantom's hooves clattered off grass and onto a firm track. As they careered along it, they flew into another mist patch. Charlie began to dread where the path might be taking her. She felt a cold sweat break out on her face. There was only one place in the Abbey grounds she did not want to be, one place that could spell instant death for Phantom...

They flew out of the disintegrating pocket of mist, and instantly Charlie could see what she and Phantom were bearing down on with every stride. Charlie's breath caught in her throat, and for a couple of strides she was frozen with fear. She didn't know how close the others were behind her, or if their ponies were bolting too. She had to warn them, but the words got stuck in her throat. Then, at the last second, she managed to squeeze them out.

"CATTLE GRID!"

Just after the gun shot, Wish's sensible nature had deserted her, and she had flown up the track like the devil was on her tail. Mia tried to get her mare back under some kind of control. But Wish had fought for her head, bunny hopping and launching herself into the air in protest. They were nearly at the end of the track, facing the new hedge before Wish finally steadied and began to calm down, even if she was still travelling at a speedy canter. Phantom, swifter than the wind, disappeared in front of her, but Mia knew that if she could slow Wish, Alice and Rosie would have more chance of getting their ponies under control, too. After she'd managed to cling on as Wish swerved violently at the hedge, she dared risk a glance over her shoulder.

"Are you two okay?" she called out. She glimpsed Alice just behind her, struggling with a headstrong Scout, and Rosie grimly hanging on for dear life to Dancer's mane. Dancer was throwing up great clods of earth with her pounding hooves; her head was low, her ears flat back to her neck, her eyes goggling.

Rosie and Alice called out that they were all right. Mia was relieved they were both still on board, but she couldn't be so sure about Charlie. Then she heard her friend yell, "Cattle grid!" and she felt her blood freeze in her veins. Cattle grids were death traps for horses. Mia passed the warning back to Rosie and Alice, then sat deep into her saddle and used all her strength to pull Wish up. Scout and Dancer almost crashed into the back of her, but it worked, and they all slowed. Then all they could do was sit and watch in horror as the pockets of mist on the path in front of them finally lifted and ahead, Phantom steered a runaway path directly towards the hideous, metallic trap.

ʊ ʊ ʊ ʊ

Charlie saw the broad, deep hole with its metallic frame, rushing up to greet her. Across the frame ran thick, solid metal poles. It was designed to stop cattle from leaving the estate grounds. But at the speed they were going, if Phantom didn't see it, his front legs would plunge straight down between the gaps. Their momentum and the weight of Phantom's body would carry him onwards, snapping his legs in an instant. It was as if everything were happening to someone else, not her.

Charlie felt fear grip her throat. Phantom had been through so much in his short life. She'd nearly lost him once before, and she wasn't about lose him now. The trouble was, she also knew there was no way she could stop Phantom in time. So Charlie did the one thing that might just save him. She sat down in the saddle and kicked for all she was worth, lifting her reins at the same time, crying, "Hup!"

The black horse's ears flickered. Then with a grunt, he was soaring into the air. Charlie tucked in close to him, not wanting for a second to unbalance her horse, or bring him down to earth before it was safe. She glanced down and saw the ugly dark hole with its great metal bars flash beneath her. Phantom arced powerfully, as if suddenly spooking from the danger beneath him. Then Charlie felt his front legs flick out, ready for landing. She desperately hoped it was far enough. She prepared herself for the jolt, and got it, almost bouncing out of the saddle as Phantom touched down on the dirt track the other side. He tipped onto his nose and scrabbled forward with his hind legs, desperately trying to get them underneath him. Charlie sat back to help as much as she could, and as soon as he recovered, Charlie squeezed on her reins. Phantom finally listened, all his fight evaporated and he skidded to a halt. Charlie felt her eyes blur, overcome by what had almost been. Without wasting a second, she turned to look for her friends.

She was just in time to see them drag their ponies to a halt on the other side of the grid. Finally, Charlie let out a long, shaky breath; her fingers were trembling like crazy on the reins. Her legs felt like jelly. For a moment they all sat where they were, unable to speak.

Mia collected herself, and called over to Charlie. "We're going to find a way over to you a bit further up."

Charlie nodded. She didn't trust herself to speak just yet, as tears of shock were suddenly welling in her eyes. She and Phantom were now standing on a lane outside the Abbey grounds, on one side of a stout hedge. There was an area further along where the hedge was a bit smaller, and the others popped their ponies over from an active trot. Even Dancer didn't think twice – she was so pumped that she flew straight over.

Once they were all on the lane, they rode over to where Charlie and Phantom were waiting. Charlie leant forward and hugged her horse around his hot neck, feeling utterly grateful that he was alive. The other three ponies were dark with sweat, and still twitchy.

"Did anyone see Mr Pyke?" Charlie whispered. "I can't believe he'd actually shoot at us like that – he must be mad! I feel like riding back in there and telling him as much, too!"

Mia could tell that, as brave as Charlie might sound, she wasn't really in the mood for going back into the Abbey grounds. Especially not to confront Mr Pyke.

"Well, it's not the first time he's taken a pot shot, is it?" Alice reminded them, shakily.

The others nodded, wondering how anyone could be so reckless.

"Come on, we'd better get the ponies back," Mia said. She meant it as much for her friends, as well as the ponies. She could see how pale the girls all looked, and knew that she must look exactly the same.

"Okay," Rosie puffed, her breath still coming in shallow gasps, "but we need to go to the village shop first."

The others stared at her, wondering if the fright had turned her a bit peculiar.

"What on earth do you want to go *there* for?" Charlie asked, wanting to get home, and see Phantom safely tucked up.

"I want to go there," Rosie said, her jaw set, looking determined, "because I think we should sign that petition against the Abbey, and I think we should sign it now."

ひ ひ ひ ひ

Rosie stepped into the shop just before it closed. She fished about in her pocket to see if she had any change hiding somewhere in the depths of her jods. She was convinced, as she walked up to the noticeboard to look for the petition, that some chocolate would settle her shaken nerves very nicely. She'd left Alice holding Dancer. Her pony had tired quickly after her exertions, and was standing with her muzzle dramatically low, almost touching the floor. Dancer's eyes were still goggly, but as Rosie disappeared inside the village shop with a ping of the door, the little pony was busy lapping up all the sympathetic pats she was getting from the other three girls.

Rosie found just enough change to buy a bar of fudge. She had planned to have a bite and share the rest with the others. Only, with Rosie distracted by the noticeboard, the fudge had disappeared bite by bite without her realising. She had found the petition and borrowed a pen from Mrs Gleeson behind the counter. Rosie flipped over the first, completely filled page, and added her and her three friends' names at the top of the next. Then she began to scan the first page to see who else had signed. Suddenly her eyes almost popped out of her head.

She dropped the pen, started to choke on the last mouthful of fudge, and rushed to the door.

"You… you…" Rosie gulped and coughed and spluttered. "You'll never… believe… this! You… have… to see it!"

Rosie dashed back inside the shop, leaving the others staring, mystified, at each other.

"I'll wait with the ponies," Charlie offered, not wanting to leave Phantom. "You two go in and see what Rosie's on about."

Mia and Alice jumped down, wincing with pain as they landed on frozen feet.

"This had better be worth it," Alice said, hobbling into the shop. Charlie stood, peering through the window, while holding all four sets of reins. The others were only inside for a few moments, before they crashed out of the door again.

"You'll never guess what," Alice said, taking Scout's reins and jumping back into the saddle.

"Just tell me!" Charlie said impatiently, handing the others back their reins and mounting again. She hated being the last to know news.

"There are loads of names on the petition,"

Mia filled her in, as she and Rosie jumped up and the four ponies started to walk the short distance home. "But, starting from the top, the first is Long Lane Livery..."

"The next is Mrs Maplethorp," Alice continued.

Charlie started. "So, the first two the people who've objected to the Abbey shutting off their rides have ended up with their ponies being let loose! It's like it's some kind of revenge or something!"

"And wait for it," Rosie pressed on. "The third name on the list is—" But Rosie didn't get a chance to finish.

"Don't tell me," Charlie jumped in, "it's Mrs Greenfield, from Greenfield's Riding School."

"Got it in one!" Rosie said, all fired up.

"So who signed the petition next, then?" Charlie asked, as the ponies pricked their ears and lengthened their stride, recognising that they were on their way home.

The others looked at each other, then at Charlie.

"Fran Hope," Alice said.

They all thought about the ragged collection of animals up at Hope Farm, every single one of them dear to Fran's heart. But for Charlie, there was one animal that was dearer than all the rest. Pirate. Her beloved first pony, whose paddock at Hope Farm sat right alongside the road…

Chapter Nine

By the time the girls got back to the yard that afternoon, the chilly darkness was already closing in. The four friends were still a bit shaken from what had happened at the Abbey, but there was no time to sit down. They led their weary ponies into the stables, and untacked, groomed and checked them thoroughly for injuries.

All Charlie wanted to do was collapse, but she knew that Phantom was her first priority. Although it was cold, Charlie stood Phantom in the yard and hosed his lower legs down with cool water. She ran her hands down them, relieved that the hard tendons down the back of his cannon bones were not showing any lumps or swellings. Then she dried his legs off, and wrapped them in stable bandages.

Each of them rugged up their ponies extra

cosily, then lugged stuffed haynets into their stables. While the ponies tucked in gratefully, the girls turned on the yard lights, and made up the feeds. They took them back to the stables, and left the ponies to finish eating in peace.

Next, it was Cracker and Frostie's turn. The girls made up more feeds, then trudged over the sheep field in the almost darkness. As they appeared by the rickety wooden railings the two horses whickered and trotted up to meet them, ears pricked. They nose dived into the buckets, eating alongside each other companionably, raising their heads to chew and have a relaxed look round.

"As soon as we get back to the yard," Alice said, "we'd better ring Fran. We need to warn her about the names on the petition list."

The others agreed, as they stood watching the two horses chomp their feed contentedly. Charlie stood, resting one gloved hand on Cracker's stocky neck. She could feel that he was toasty and warm in his rugs. Once Cracker had finished, Charlie bent down and scooped the last morsels of food from the curve of the feed bucket, and swished it into the middle. Cracker nudged her hand out of the way, and greedily lipped the last few mouthfuls.

"I know it might sound horrible," Charlie said, "but I don't want these two to go to Fran's now, not if there's any chance that Hope Farm might be targeted next by the Abbey, or Billy at least. I'd hate for anything to happen to either of them."

"Me too," Rosie agreed, quickly. "Can't we ask Fran if they can stay here? I can see if Dad can fix that spare stable."

But Mia, forever the sensible one, shook her head. "That stable won't get mended overnight," she pointed out, "and this field is seriously insecure. All we can do is let Fran know what we suspect, don't you think?"

The others agreed, reluctantly.

Mr Honeycott had been out and topped up the horses' hay and water earlier in the day, so after the girls had hugged the horses goodnight, they headed back to the yard. By now, it was dark, and the Christmas lanterns flickered and the tinsel sparkled under the bright stable lights. But instead of heading towards the stables, the girls made their way to the hay barn. They picked out their way by torchlight and bundled in, climbing the ladder into the loft. The barn sat just behind the stables, overlooking the paddocks. From there, they could just about hear their ponies when they snorted, or stomped a hoof.

The Pony Detectives snuggled down amongst the hay bales. Rosie had sneaked some freshly made cinnamon rolls from the farmhouse kitchen, and as they huddled together and ate, they finally started to warm up. There was a sudden pitter patter of light footsteps and Rosie flashed the torch round in the dark. Pumpkin's green eyes blazed, and he meowed as he headed over, looking for a toasty lap to curl up on. He chose Rosie's. She wrapped the blanket around him, as well as herself, tucking it under his chin.

Charlie held the torch as Mia pulled out her phone. Mia's fingers were almost too frozen to activate the screen, but she managed to tap in Fran's number and press Call. Then she put her phone on speaker and gave Fran an update. She didn't mention that they'd sneaked into the Abbey grounds, and had the fright of their lives, or overheard Billy and Archie's argument. But Fran didn't sound overly convinced by the connection the girls were making between the petition list and the horses being let loose.

"I'm sure it's just a coincidence," Fran sighed. "Although… the local gossip *is* that Billy Pyke might be involved with what happened at Greenfields last night. According to some, he's done this kind of thing before… Anyway, I will keep an extra eye out, petition list or no petition list. Luckily we've got enough barns here to move all the horses and ponies into them overnight. The weather's so bitter at the moment that I was half thinking about doing that anyway. It's more work, but I don't think the horses will mind too much."

Mia felt an instant flood of relief, knowing that if the horses at Hope Farm were kept in overnight, they'd be safe.

"Now, about this Friday," Fran continued. "My lorry's being serviced at the garage, so I'll have to lead Cracker and Frostie in hand. Fancy helping?"

"Of course we will," Mia said. Even though she was happier that Cracker and Frostie wouldn't be out in the fields at their new home, she still couldn't quite manage to feel happy about them going. It already felt like Blackberry Farm would be too quiet without them. But she also knew that the horses couldn't stay on the common land forever.

"Perfect," Fran said. "In that case I'll see you this Friday at 10 a.m. And try not to worry about Pirate, or the other horses. Like I said, I've got eyes all over the place at the moment, believe me."

After Mia ended the call, she grabbed her notebook from under one of the hay bales. She slid out a pen, which she kept pushed down inside the notebook's spiral binding wire, and removed the lid.

"So, we've got three mysteries," Mia recapped, running her finger over the clues already written on the page. "The first is Cracker and Frostie."

"And all we've got on that is the half a footprint clue," Rosie said, reading over Mia's shoulder. "And a tyre track."

"And the fact that someone dumped them in the middle of the night," Charlie added.

"Then there's the mystery of the horses escaping from Long Lane, Mrs Maplethorp's and Greenfields," Alice said.

All the girls brightened at mention of this one, because there was more to go on. Mia flattened out the newspaper article on the hay bale in front of them, which had reported Mrs Maplethorp's ponies getting out of their paddocks.

"A powerful motorbike's been heard at each place where ponies have been set loose," Charlie said. "And we found out today that Billy's got a motorbike."

"On top of that, Billy's got a history of doing this kind of stuff, too," Alice added, "according to Mr Perryvale's hints, at least, and local gossip."

"And we know Archie found something at Greenfield's Riding School, in the grass right next to the field where the ponies were let out," Mia said, scribbling down notes. "We just don't know what. But I bet it was something that pointed towards Billy being guilty, judging by Archie's reaction."

"And Billy wanted Archie to keep something a secret from Nick and Mr Pyke," Alice said, "which makes it sound like Billy's acting without their help."

"Although half the village seem to be pinning the blame on Billy," Charlie added. "So I don't really see how he could keep it a secret from Nick for long."

"Don't forget that the owners of each place that has been targeted so far have signed a petition to get rides at the Abbey reopened," Rosie continued, playing with Pumpkin's soft ears. "So, that points the finger of blame directly at someone from the Abbey. Add that to our other clues, and that someone *has* to be Billy."

Charlie nodded. "We all heard Billy saying to Archie that he couldn't afford to let the Abbey polo club fail. Maybe he's trying to scare everyone into dropping the petition so they leave the Abbey alone."

Mia paused for a second in her writing. "But that doesn't actually add up, does it?" she said, scratching the tip of her nose with the end of the pen. "Frightening everyone on that petition list is not the way to increase the club's popularity round here."

"Exactly," Alice sighed. "All that would do is turn everyone against the Abbey even more. That's the exact *opposite* of what Nick Webb wanted. He had hoped everyone would be part of the Abbey."

"Well, he *said* that," Charlie pointed out, "but as soon as he brought the ponies to the yard he started blocking off the Abbey rides, without telling anyone why."

"And that leads to the third mystery," Rosie said. "Why has Nick Webb suddenly changed his mind about the Abbey rides? What made him close them off, and why is he letting Mr Pyke shoot at riders to keep them away?"

The girls sat in silence for a moment, deep in thought.

"Well, maybe something happened after he moved into the Abbey to make him change his mind," Alice finally said. "It's the only explanation."

"But we're still no closer to finding out *what*," Charlie sighed.

The wind whistled outside, rattling the barn walls and sending snakes of icy air in through the gaps. The girls snuggled deeper into their blankets for a second.

Rosie looked at the newspaper again. She skimmed through it, then frowned.

"What's up?" Alice asked, hunkering down further into her blanket.

Rosie used her cinnamon roll to point at the words. "It says there a *powerful* motorbike."

"So?" Charlie asked.

"Well, I don't know much about motorbikes," Rosie shrugged, "but I didn't think Billy's bike sounded that powerful at all…"

The others looked at each other, quizzically.

"No, it's got to be Billy," Mia said decisively. "Him letting the horses out of their fields is the one mystery we *are* sure about."

"*That* bit might make sense," Charlie said, feeling impatient, "but we're only guessing at why Billy's let the horses out. And we still don't know what's made Nick Webb change his mind about keeping the rides open. What if Alice is right, and something's happened inside the Abbey grounds?"

"If that is the case, the only thing we can do," Rosie sighed, "is head back for another poke about, see if we can unearth anything."

The four of them sat glumly in the torch-lit silence. These were the first mysteries that the Pony Detectives wished they hadn't got involved with. But before they had a chance to say as much out loud to each other, the barn door creaked open. A pale face loomed into view, spooking them so much that they squealed in fright and nearly fell off their hay bales.

"Charlie, your dad's here," Rosie's brother Will called out, grinning into the darkness.

Acting like they hadn't been scared, the girls raced out of the barn and back to the yard. After shouting out a goodbye to Rosie, the others piled into Charlie's car.

On the way home, Charlie's dad chatted away to them about their last week at school, and about Christmas. But their minds were miles away, filled with thoughts about motorbikes, escaping ponies and secrets locked deep within the Abbey grounds.

The final week at school passed in a blur. There was a Christmas carol concert held in the main hall, cards exchanged on the school bus and in class, a school play and a non-uniform day. Everyone was in really high spirits except India and Archie. The pair had kept themselves to themselves the whole week, not even joining in with the high spirited banter on the bus. It hadn't helped that Sophie and some of the other horsey girls had been overheard chatting loudly about Billy Pyke, and how everyone suspected he was the one letting all the ponies out of their fields.

Alice had felt terrible for Archie, especially when she noticed him look round anxiously at India. India had given him a stare in return which was half way between sympathetic and a warning, and he'd turned back, saying nothing. The only good thing was that at least Sophie had looked mortified when she'd realised Archie had overheard.

But India looked down in the dumps on the last day of term, too, despite the fact that they were breaking up at lunchtime. The Pony Detectives didn't get it. They couldn't wait to have the chance to spend some extra time with Cracker and Frostie, before their relocation to Hope Farm the next day.

"What's up?" one of India's best friends asked as India slumped down on her seat in the school bus. "You've been miserable all week – did someone forget to tell you it was Christmas?"

The Pony Detectives stopped chattering amongst themselves, and began to eavesdrop on the conversation.

"It's just horsey stuff," India sighed. "Rumour had a fall last Sunday when I was hacking in the Abbey grounds. The vet said she's twisted her knee. We ice packed it and cold hosed it, but the vet's ruled her out of the Winter Cup. I don't suppose you know of any polo ponies that are all trained up and ready to go, do you? Oh, and cheap as chips, too. Dad can't afford much at the moment."

"Sorry, India," her friend joked, "I'm right out of polo ponies just now."

India struggled to raise a smile.

"Looks like my team's chances of even competing in the Winter Cup, let alone winning it, are getting slimmer by the day," India sighed. "Stormchaser's our only real hope. I just hope *he* doesn't get injured between now and New Year's Eve. Otherwise our very first attempt at hosting an event at the Abbey will be a complete washout. None of the other big clubs will take us seriously."

"I doubt anyone will bother to turn up, anyway," one of Sophie's friends from Greenfield's Riding School said under her breath, just loud enough for the Pony Detectives to hear.

Charlie and Mia turned round to look through the gap in the seats at Rosie and Alice.

All of them were feeling uneasy about India's latest revelation.

"That's the second pony injured at the Abbey in a week," Charlie whispered, keeping her voice low so that Archie couldn't hear. "First, Thimble twisted his fetlock, now Rumour's strained her knee!"

"And India's scared about Stormchaser getting injured," Rosie added under her breath. "What is going *on* in that place?"

"I don't know," Alice grimaced, "but at this rate, with Billy letting horses out of fields, Mr Pyke taking pot shots at riders and all those injuries, I don't think the Abbey can possibly make it as a successful polo club."

"Well, let's hope not, anyway," Mia said, "for the sake of every pony round here."

At that moment the bus came to a stop, just before it reached the Abbey entrance. While some of the pupils carried on chatting, others wiped the windows to get a better look at what was happening outside. A woman leading two smart chestnut polo ponies along the lane and into the Abbey grounds was just about visible.

India instantly perked up, dashing to the front of the bus and grabbing Archie on the way past. "Come on, Archie," she said breezily. "Look! Maddie's moving into the Abbey! Dad said she was *thinking* of switching her polo ponies to our club, from Perryvale's, but it looks like she actually *has*! Great news!"

"Is it?" Archie said, looking more worried than delighted.

The bus driver opened the doors and the pair jumped down, amidst shouts of 'Happy Christmas'. Archie dragged his bag behind him following India into the Abbey grounds.

"That's weird," Mia said, tilting her head to one side for a moment as the bus pulled away and excited chatter filled the air again.

"What is?" Charlie asked.

"It's just that with everything that's been going on recently," Mia replied, "why would *anyone* want to move from Mr Perryvale's polo yard to the Abbey?"

"If you want my opinion," Rosie said, "the world of polo is utterly mad."

"Too right," Sophie piped up.

The Pony Detectives looked at each other. As enthusiastic as they'd been to get involved a few weeks ago, things had changed dramatically since then. The polo yard seemed to lurk at the centre of their mysteries, like a menacing shadow. They were convinced that something sinister was going on there, but they weren't sure they wanted to find out what.

Chapter Ten

Fran Hope appeared promptly at ten o' clock the next morning. It was cold out, but the sky was a bright blue and the sun was shining.

The Pony Detectives had got to the yard extra early, to make sure Cracker and Frostie were sparkling and ready to go to Hope Farm. They had also spent most of their free afternoon the day before grooming and petting them, bringing them into the yard, where they could tie them up outside the stables. Their coats hadn't been groomed for ages, and bits of their winter fluff came out in chunks and drifted across the yard. When Fran arrived at the Blackberry Farm gate, the girls had mixed emotions about saying goodbye.

"They've put on a good bit of weight already. They look magnificent!" Fran said, smiling broadly as she cast her expert eye over them.

"They've been trained, and loved – that much I'd guess. Who on earth would want to dump them? We'll probably never know... Anyway, let's get them going."

The girls insisted on taking it in turns to lead Cracker and Frostie. They walked out of Blackberry Farm calmly, with Charlie and Mia flanking Cracker in the lead, while Rosie and Alice walked either side of Frostie just behind. He'd begun to settle, and was now almost as relaxed as Cracker, but he'd never be as bold. When he accidentally trod on the back of Rosie's welly boot, he nudged her, looking apologetic. Rosie rested her arm over his neck for a few strides, letting him know he was forgiven. Fran strode along at the head of the little line, looking out for potential spooks, like dogs waiting at gateways, ready to burst out barking.

The horses kept their rugs on for the chilly walk along the lanes. The girls were wrapped up warmly but their noses and cheeks still turned red, and their toes froze before they'd even reached half way.

"We'll have a hot drink when we get to the Farm," Fran said, walking backwards for a few strides and admiring the horses' calm steps, "once these two are settled in."

"My stomach's rumbling already," Rosie moaned, as they marched along at the horses' speed, "I should've bought some of Mum's cinnamon rolls to eat on the way."

"I'm sure I can find something in one of the cupboards for you," Fran smiled, knowing Rosie well, "if you can hang on that long."

"The cross country route would have been much quicker," Rosie pointed out. "We'd nearly be there by now."

Fran had decided that it would be safer and easier to take the horses along the lanes. There would be less to spook them in the hedgerows and they wouldn't be stumbling over rutted, iron hard earth. This longer route took them in the direction of the Perryvale and Abbey estates, and as they mooched along one of the nearby lanes, they heard a smooth engine purring behind them. As they turned to look, the Perryvale Range Rover pulled up alongside. Rosie noticed that the big splodge from Dancer's lick on the bonnet had been meticulously polished off.

Mr Perryvale's cool gaze took in the two horses, as he cruised along slowly. He lowered his window and waved to Fran. The unmistakable smell of stale cigars wafted out.

"Not more escaped horses?" Mr Perryvale asked, knitting his eyebrows in concern.

"Luckily not," Fran smiled back. "Although I say luckily, I'm not quite sure that's the case. These two were abandoned a couple of weeks ago."

Mr Perryvale nodded. "I see," he said, his voice neutral as his eyes ran over the horses. "Are you all right walking?" he asked, as a smile formed on his well rounded face. "Or can I offer you a lift anywhere? I'm sure I could rustle up a trailer if needed? Have you got far to go?"

"To the Farm, but it's not too much further thanks," Fran said cheerily. "And these two are angels to lead. Anyway, the exercise is good."

"Who for?" Rosie whispered under her breath, making Alice giggle. Her feet were starting to ache too, with a combination of being worn out and frozen all at the same time.

"Fair enough, although rather you than me," Mr Perryvale said, taking a puff on his cigar, before giving another wave and disappearing up the lane.

"He doesn't look like *he* gets much exercise," Charlie smiled to Mia. "I wouldn't want to be his polo pony."

"Charlie…" Fran remonstrated, but only half-heartedly. "It's not entirely his fault. He had a riding accident a few years back and broke his ankle badly. I think he can ride better now than he can walk! Well, that's what he tells me, anyway. Not that I know him well, mind you. It's only recently that he's even spoken to me, which is odd, considering we've lived in the same village for years. He's always been far too lah-di-dah for the likes of scruffy old me."

As they carried on up the lane, past the entrance to the Abbey grounds, Charlie's attention was suddenly brought back to Cracker, who had lifted his head, his ears pricked. Alice noticed Frostie's head bob up, too. For the first time, the two horses became slightly jumpy, and their stride more urgent. They stayed restless as they approached the next corner, their ears pricked.

As they got nearer, the girls could hear the metallic clatter of lots of hooves clopping along the lane. They could hear one set of hooves skidding and then a pause followed by another skid, as if the pony the hooves belonged to was dancing and leaping along the lane.

"I still don't think this little pony will be ready in time," a girl's voice called out despondently. "She kept shying away from the stick and the ball this morning during the practice chukka."

"Well, she'll have to play in *one* of the chukkas, inexperienced or not," a heavily accented, slightly out of breath male voice called back.

"We haven't got much choice anyway, since the other ponies are dropping like flies," a third, deeper voice added.

Charlie turned to Mia. "That sounds like India, and Estoni, doesn't it?"

Mia nodded. "*And* Billy, I think!"

Fran hollered out at the front of their ride, giving the riders and ponies around the corner an advance warning of their presence. She held up her hand, and the girls halted Cracker and Frostie, who jittered on the spot, their ears hard forward.

Around the corner appeared the bull-like bay Stormchaser, with Estoni on top. Close up, his choppy stride, thick set neck and chest made him look even more intimidating and terrifying, especially now there were no arena walls to contain him. He started, but for a moment paused in the lane, his whole body quivering like a bomb that was about to go off.

Behind Estoni and Stormchaser followed two more riders. Each was mounted on a pony, and leading two more. The girls recognised Billy Pyke beneath his polo helmet, and just behind him was India Webb, sitting on a steel grey polo pony. Their faces were a picture of surprise as they almost bumped into Fran and the girls.

Cracker took a step forward. Charlie grabbed his head collar, not fancying being dragged any closer to the tank-like Stormchaser. But Cracker pulled forward again, leaning towards Stormchaser, and giving a soft whinny. To the girls' amazement, Stormchaser responded with a soft whicker. Alice jumped when Frostie joined in, right in her ear. At the front, Estoni looked confused as he studied the two horses in front of him.

"Thunder...? Misty?" He said.

"Er..." Charlie began, but at that moment, Stormchaser's quivering halt exploded. He'd clearly waited long enough and he set off at a head-fighting canter down the lane.

"I see you back at the Abbey!" Estoni called over his shoulder, sitting lightly in the saddle as he tried to contain the bay pony beneath him.

"Okay!" India shouted back.

Her grey polo pony began to scrape the ground and try to move forward, unsettled by Stormchaser's antics. India struggled to hold her, the other ponies either side of her and the two sets of reins in her hands. When they had calmed slightly, she turned her attention back to the horses in front of her.

"Where are those two off to?"

"Hope Farm," Fran replied.

"*Hope Farm*?" India repeated, her face a mixture of surprise and bewilderment. "How come?"

"Abandoned," Fran called back, "dumped."

A flash of anger crossed Billy's face, and Alice noticed India glance at him.

"No one's claimed them yet," Fran continued, "so they're coming to mine, then I can see about rehoming them. Why, are you interested?"

Billy managed a humourless smile. "You never know."

India's young grey horse snorted and took a few steps back, shaking her head.

"We'd better get going," Billy said, with the slightest of nods to India. "We don't want another accident. Come on."

Everyone said goodbye, then India and Billy set off with their six polo ponies.

Cracker and Frostie stepped on reluctantly.

"Why would they be exercising their polo ponies on the lanes when they've got so much estate to ride in?" Mia puzzled quietly to the others as Fran strode ahead to check there were no cars coming round the corner.

"I don't know," Charlie shook her head. "It seems like a crazy thing to do, especially with a pony like Stormchaser."

Rosie frowned. "Unless the Abbey isn't safe for them, either? Billy mentioned that ponies were dropping like flies, before he realised we were there…"

Alice had a quick glimpse over her shoulder before they reached the corner. She baulked as she noticed Billy, turned in his saddle slightly. He was watching her and her friends, and the two horses. She could feel his gaze remain upon them until they headed round the bend in the lane and disappeared from view.

The Pony Detectives stayed at Hope Farm for ages, helping to settle Cracker and Frostie into their new home. They fussed about, checking rugs, fluffing up hay piles in the new field, and double checking the water buckets were clean and full. Once they'd finished, Fran showed them the stables the horses would be brought into each night.

"Old Mouse and Marlee will be okay out in the barns with Pirate and the small group in there," Fran said.

Then, after cups of tea and plenty of hugs for Cracker and Frostie, the girls climbed into Mr Honeycott's pick-up truck for their lift back to the farm.

With no feeds to lug over to the common land, or water to change, or hay to spread out, the late afternoon stable chores were over far too quickly. So instead they spent ages hanging out with their own ponies, and talking about the Christmas outfits they'd wear to Fran's charity ride on the twenty-third of December, the day after next.

"Well, there's no way I'm dressing Phantom up," Charlie grinned. "If I put reindeer antlers on him I'll probably get a repeat performance of that bolt I had up the Abbey track!"

"I've got a bunch of pink tinsel to wrap around me and Wish," Mia grinned, getting excited already about the hack.

"I hope it's not too dull if it's just all round the roads," Rosie groaned. "I feel like that's all we've done recently. The tracks through the Abbey are pretty much the only safe woodland ones that don't freeze up."

"*Were* the only safe ones," Alice corrected her. "Anyway, even if it is all road work, it's still for a good cause."

While they waited in the stables for Charlie's mum to turn up, they quickly texted Fran, to find out how Cracker and Frostie were settling in.

They're delightful, but won't be here long! New home found for them together ALREADY. Will update you at Charity Ride!

"I can't believe it!" Alice said, happily. "And they get to stay together, too!"

"I want to know more *right now*," Rosie said, urgently, feeling the excitement bubble up inside her, "it'll feel like forever waiting 'til we see Fran at the ride!"

"If the ride goes ahead, that is," Mia said, gesturing outside. The mist was starting to roll in again, glowing silver in the late afternoon light. "If this stuff doesn't clear there won't even *be* a ride."

Charlie suddenly felt a shiver. "It was misty when the Greenfield ponies were let loose, wasn't it?"

The others thought for a moment, then Mia nodded. "And it was mentioned in the paper, when Mrs Maplethorp's gates were opened."

"When Cracker and Frostie were abandoned," Alice added, "it was misty then, too…"

"It could be coincidence, couldn't it?" Rosie frowned.

"Fran's got all her horses safe in barns, remember," Mia said, trying to sound positive. "And Rosie's right, it could just be a coincidence."

At that moment Charlie's mum's car pulled up. The girls said goodbye, and left the yard reluctantly. Their own ponies may have been safely tucked up in their stables, but they still felt uneasy about what new disaster the silver mist might leave in its wake.

Chapter
Eleven

CHARLIE had taken ages to fall asleep. She'd been looking outside her window every five minutes. Not that it had helped. The mist had grown thicker, making her more and more unsettled. When she was woken by the insistent, brash ring of her phone, the room was still pitch black.

"Neve?" Charlie yawned, rolling over as she answered the call. She felt all disorientated, wondering why Pirate's loaner would be calling her in the middle of the night. "What's up?"

Charlie's yawn ended abruptly as she heard the panic in the voice at the other end of the phone. She was sitting upright in a second, her heart drumming inside her chest so hard that she thought it might explode. Only one thought was in her head.

"Pirate!" Charlie gulped. "Is he okay?"

Charlie was struggling to piece together Neve's desperate words, but with a sickening dread she realised that Hope Farm had been broken into, and horses set loose. Pirate was fine, *his* barn hadn't been broken into, but Neve's next words made Charlie's heart pound even harder.

"Some of the horses in the *stables* were let out?" Charlie gasped. This was a new development – until now horses had been let out of *fields*. But stables…? Suddenly it dawned on her what Neve was getting to. She felt her stomach flip upside down, but she still wasn't prepared for the news that was about to hit her.

Neve's voice began to crack, and she became tearful. Charlie didn't want to hear what Neve was saying, but she couldn't block the words out. Cracker and Frostie, along with another couple of horses had been let out of their stables. A motorbike had been heard, circling and revving its engine hard. Neve wasn't sure if it was just to make a quick getaway, or a deliberate attempt to scare the horses. Either way, they'd bolted, scattering onto the lanes. By the time

Fran had found them, it was too late. About two miles away towards town, in thick mist on a blind corner, she'd discovered Frostie, who was quivering by the verge. Cracker lay beside him in the road. A lorry driver had been kneeling by the handsome bay horse's head. Cracker's eyes were open, but they'd never see again. He was dead.

Charlie couldn't sleep for the rest of the night. She didn't know how she would manage to find the words to tell the others. The following morning, she turned up at Blackberry Farm with puffy eyes, still numb. Alice wouldn't believe her, even though she knew it must be true from Charlie's face. Rosie bit her lip hard, but couldn't keep the tears from tumbling down her face and even Mia, who was normally so composed, sat heavily at the kitchen table, too stunned to talk.

Mrs Honeycott dabbed her eyes a couple of times as she made the girls hot, sweet drinks.

Will sat awkwardly at the table. He looked like he wanted an excuse to leave the kitchen, and seconds later he nipped out to feed the waiting ponies in the yard without the girls even having to ask. Mr Honeycott offered to run the girls home and sort out the stables himself, but all they wanted was to be with their ponies.

On the way to Dancer's stable, Rosie saw some tufts of brown hair, mixed with white, blown to the edge of the tack room. She bent and picked them up. It was Cracker and Frostie's hair, from when the girls had groomed them the day before. Rosie stroked it, hardly able to believe that less than twenty-four hours earlier, Cracker had stood in that very spot, quietly being brushed and fussed over, ahead of Fran's arrival. Now everything had changed. Mia came and stood next to her friend. Rosie's body shook with a huge, jagged sigh. She gave a tuft of the brown hair to Mia. They both slipped them into their pockets before heading to their ponies.

Wish was at the stable door, looking for Mia. The mare's huge dark-brown, long lashed eyes looked sad, as if Wish was sensing Mia's mood. Wish stretched out her muzzle, and blew warm breath through her nostrils over Mia's face, tickling Mia with her whiskers. The mare briefly rested her chin on Mia's shoulder. When Mia let herself into her pony's stable, she slid her hands under Wish's blanket, taking comfort from her pony's warmth. Wish stood quietly and for a moment, a peaceful hush fell over the stables. But the silence didn't last long.

"Ow, Dancer!" Rosie squawked indignantly, through her tears. "There really is nothing stashed away under my hat!"

Rosie let herself out of Dancer's stable, and let herself into Wish's, rubbing her forehead.

"I hope your pony's better at giving sympathy than Dancer," Rosie grumbled as she gently tapped Wish's muzzle. "She never misses an opportunity to rummage for a treat, no matter what the occasion."

"A bit like her owner, then," Alice said with a half sniff, half laugh as she let herself out of Scout's stable, and into Wish's, too. Charlie joined them, looking puzzled.

"What's up?" Rosie asked, wiping her dripping nose on her glove.

"Neve just called," Charlie said. "I texted to ask if she knew who Fran had lined up as Cracker and Frostie's new owners. She called me straightaway." Charlie took a deep breath. Even saying Cracker's name bought a fresh lump to her throat.

"And?" Alice asked. Yesterday they couldn't wait to find out, but now Alice wasn't sure she even really wanted to know, because if it was somewhere perfect, it would make Cracker's death even more painful to bear.

Charlie sighed, screwing up her face slightly. "Well, you might not believe this," she said, "but it was Nick Webb. Nick went with Billy to see Fran about both horses yesterday afternoon, before all this happened. Fran said they'd already decided to have them before they'd even seen them close up. Nick was going to give a generous donation for them too, apparently. So, once the twenty-one day notice had run out, they were both destined to go to the Abbey to be polo ponies. Because Thimble's injured,

Cracker was going to be one of Estoni's rides in some of the chukkas to give Stormchaser a breather and Frostie was going to India as a stand-in for Rumour in the Winter Cup. They were all really excited."

The girls looked at each other, bewildered.

"How do they even know they'd be any good at polo?" Alice asked. "They can't train them *that* quickly, can they?"

Charlie shrugged. "It doesn't make sense either way. If Nick said he wanted them, why would Billy return later that very same evening and let them both out, knowing that something bad could happen to them?"

"I... I know it's going to be really difficult," Mia said, taking a deep breath, "but I really think we should ride over to Hope Farm. I think we need to see if there are any clues, this time without Archie on hand to clear away any evidence."

The girls were glad of something positive to do. Sitting around had only made things feel ten times worse. But grooming their ponies, getting tacked up and riding over to Hope Farm felt like they were at least doing something to work out what was behind Cracker's death, and all the other field break-ins.

The mist had cleared once more, leaving its icy mark on the countryside. The sky was bright blue, the sun high. But the girls couldn't take pleasure in the wintry, frost-dusted lanes, knowing that Cracker would never enjoy the sun on his back, ever again. They took the quicker, cross-country route over the rutted fields from Blackberry Farm, rather than sticking to the lanes. They were desperate to reach Fran's, fuelled with a fresh determination to solve the mystery. But they had to take it steady over the rough ground, especially after Scout stumbled and almost went down on his nose.

They finally arrived at Hope Farm's gates, their faces set grimly. They looked for Frostie as soon as they'd jumped off their ponies. A pinched, frightened appaloosa face bobbed over the stable door. Frostie let out a low, anxious whicker and the girls rushed over to give him the biggest hug they could, their sadness resurfacing.

Neve came running out of the annexe to meet them. She showed them the motorbike tyre marks in the bare earth near the gate at the base of the drive. Neve was about to leave them to it, and head back to the main house to see if Fran needed any help, when Alice stopped her for a moment.

"Did you hear the motorbike last night?" Alice asked, glancing up and seeing that the annexe where Neve lived was set slightly closer to the lane than Fran's house.

Neve flushed. "I did," she said slowly. "But not until it was too late. I heard the revving and horses squealing, and I was out of bed in a second. I flew downstairs but by the time I was out of the front door I could hear hooves on the lane and… and the bike had gone."

"Was it a growly, powerful revving?" Rosie asked. "Or a thin, tinny sort of sound?"

Neve looked at Rosie like she was mad. "Does it matter?"

Rosie looked uncertain. "It might do."

Neve thought hard. "It was kind of deep and rumbly, and really loud. Does that help?"

The Pony Detectives looked at each other, feeling confused. Rosie had asked the right question – Neve's description really didn't sound much like Billy's motorbike.

"Did you see or hear anything else?" Charlie pressed.

Neve shook her head. "Sorry, no. Look, I'd better be getting back to Fran." She sighed heavily and headed off to the main house.

Alice was still standing and looking from the tyre marks by the lane to the annexe.

"What's up?" Mia asked, knowing that Alice was putting something together in her mind, and wishing that she could see it too.

"Well, everyone talks about how powerful this motorbike is," Alice said, one hand on her hip, the other holding Scout's reins. "And in the dead of night, it'd sound even louder. Wouldn't it have woken Neve up as it arrived? She wouldn't *just* have heard it as it was leaving, after the horses were already loose, would she?"

"What, so you think that someone might have wheeled it here," Charlie said, screwing up her face, "then only started the engine up once the horses were let loose?"

Alice shrugged, not quite sure what it was she was thinking.

"But why not just roll the bike away with the engine off in that case?" Charlie countered. "Otherwise, by starting up the engine, Billy might as well advertise that he was at each yard. He can't be that crazy, can he?"

Rosie let Dancer crop the few green shoots of grass by the edge of the Hope Farm drive. The cobby pony wandered to the end of her reins. "If you ask me, it's crazy that *anyone* would use a motorbike to sneak around on in the middle of the night, anyway," Rosie said.

Mia face lit up. "That's true! Why *would* anyone use a noisy motorbike if they didn't want to be caught?"

The girls looked at each other, feeling more tied up in knots than ever with what was happening. Suddenly they heard running footsteps and saw Neve heading back towards them, pulling something out of her pocket.

"I meant to show you this… I don't know if this is important or not," she explained and handed Charlie a red, shiny wrapper.

The girls gasped, recognising the wrapper instantly. "This is from the Abbey café!" Rosie squeaked.

"Where did you find it?" Charlie breathed.

"On the drive, earlier," Neve explained. "I thought it was rubbish, so I picked it up and put it in my pocket to chuck in the bin. Only, I forgot all about it until just now."

At that moment, Fran called over for Neve's help, so she quickly said her goodbyes, making the girls promise they'd let her know of any progress they made. After hasty reassurances, the Pony Detectives swiftly turned their attention back to the wrapper in Charlie's grasp.

"I wonder if this is what Archie found at Greenfield's," Mia said, "and what Billy was arguing about with Archie last Sunday?"

"I bet it was!" Charlie said triumphantly. "This seals it. It *has* to be Billy! Come on, we've got stacks of evidence against him now, what are we waiting for? He might be trying to sneak round intimidating everyone on that petition without the Abbey finding out, but I think

Nick Webb deserves to know exactly what his precious polo player has been up to!"

Charlie gathered her reins, feeling fired up and furious. She was about to mount, when Mia raised her hand.

"Hang on a second," Mia said quickly. "Isn't this just like the motorbike clue? Isn't it just a bit, I don't know, *too* obvious? Billy might as well have knocked at the door and introduced himself. I think there's something more going on here than we're seeing."

"Like what?" Charlie demanded, fed up of feeling stumped. She wanted answers, and fast, after what had happened to Cracker.

"That's the bit I don't know," Mia confessed, as frustrated as Charlie by their lack of progress. It was really bugging her that they seemed to be stuck in reverse.

The girls stood shivering in the arctic breeze as their ponies began to get restless.

"Well, we're not likely to come up with any amazing revelations standing here," Rosie said. "My brain is *literally* going to freeze any second, and then I won't be able to think at all."

"I've got an idea, though," Mia suggested, her eyes lighting up. "How about we pay the Perryvale Polo Club a visit on our way home? If we could speak to Mr Perryvale again, maybe he could tell us more about the last time Billy got caught letting out horses. You know, like who caught him, or why he did it. It might give us a lead in this case!"

"And Mr Perryvale's been really helpful so far," Alice added. "I'm sure he'd be okay about us asking."

"His grooms must be nice, too," Mia reasoned, "because they helped take back the Greenfield's ponies."

"Ooooh!" Rosie suddenly brightened. "And he's really rich, isn't he?"

"Yes, but what's that got to do with anything?" Mia asked.

"We can ask him to sponsor us for the Charity Ride at the same time!" Rosie smiled.

Charlie nodded, squeezing Phantom and setting off. "Right then, let's ride over to the Perryvale Polo Club. We've got to do *something*."

Rosie and Mia jumped back into their

saddles, and called out a goodbye to Neve. They were just about to set out for the Perryvale estate, when something about the gatepost at the entrance to Hope Farm caught Alice's eye. It was slanted slightly sideways. Near the top was a curved dent, like a horse had kicked out at it. She frowned, and looked towards the base of the post. And there, lying in the ground, was a yellowy orange fragment.

Alice quickly slid back out of the saddle and picked up the hard, thin plastic. It was a triangle shape, with a sliver of black lettering on it. The edge was splintered. There was a dark scuff on it, like it had been caught by a hoof too.

"What is it?" Rosie asked. Alice couldn't keep a sad smile off her face.

"It looks like part of a number plate," Alice said, looking up. "I reckon a horse kicked out at the bike last night, and caught both the post and the bike. I wouldn't be surprised if it was Cracker, trying to protect Frostie."

"And if it was," Mia added, "Cracker might just have left us the biggest clue to solving who's behind this mystery, once and for all."

Chapter
Twelve

Mia had felt quite grand, as she led the others on the ride up the long drive to Mr Perryvale's country house. The drive was lined with evenly spaced, leafless poplar trees, the tips of their branches tinged with a white frost. The trees bent lightly in the chill wind. Farmland stretched either side of the driveway. At the very edge of the landscape on her left, she could see the rise of the Abbey ruins above dense boundary hedges. Polo ponies, with neatly hogged manes and wearing smart royal blue rugs, lifted their heads to watch the four ponies ride past. The paddocks looked well kept, recently pooh-picked and furnished with piles of hay.

The girls continued up the drive and approached the impressive house. Mia frowned, noticing that some of the curtains were old and tired-looking. The house looked like it could do with a good paint, too. She started to feel uneasy, and she wondered if Mr Perryvale would be happy about them just turning up out of the blue at his private yard. The girls stood for a second, wondering which way to go, but they could hear the sound of forks scraping stable floors and a radio blasting out music.

They headed towards the noise, which was coming from the back of the house. Beyond a grand wall stood what looked to Mia like it had once been a magnificent yard. Big, brick built stables stood around a large square of neatly clipped grass. A tall tower with a white clock face rose opposite them, incorporated into the stables. But the clock showed the wrong time and half the smart stables were empty.

At the sound of hoof beats, various pony heads looked towards them, and others came to the front of their stables.

Mia looked beyond the stables to the paddocks behind. She couldn't help feeling surprised and disappointed; the ponies turned out there had ancient-looking rugs, some of which had rips in. The paddocks themselves looked bare and they hadn't been pooh-picked for ages. There was no hay in sight. Behind the smart exterior, the exclusive Perryvale Polo Club didn't look so exclusive after all. Instead it looked jaded and rundown. It wasn't at all what she'd been expecting to find, and it didn't match up with the image given off by Mr Perryvale and his shiny Range Rover.

Mia turned back to the stables. The yard's emptiness gave it an eerie feel.

"This isn't quite what I expected," Mia whispered, looking round. The others nodded in agreement, shivering as they stood rigid in the icy wind.

A groom looked out from one of the stable doors. He let himself out of his stable, and Mia caught sight of dark, dank-looking bedding inside. The groom carried a broom with almost completely worn bristles as he walked towards the new arrivals. He was wearing a royal blue Perryvale Polo Club jacket. As he got nearer, the girls could see that he looked flashy, with thick, dark hair, sun-kissed skin and electric blue eyes. He didn't smile as he approached. The girls stood awkwardly, wishing they could be transported straight out of the yard. But it was too late to turn around and trot off now.

"Can I help you?" the groom asked coldly, as he stopped just in front of them. He stood close to Wish, and something about him made Mia want to ask him to step back from her pony. Wish raised her head slightly, and flicked her ears back, like she felt the same.

"We were hoping to talk to Mr Perryvale," Mia explained, feeling her nerve start to waver slightly under the groom's unflinchingly cold stare.

"He's not here," the groom said bluntly. "Is he expecting you?"

The girls shook their heads. "No," Charlie said. "But we were hoping to find out more about Billy Pyke letting out horses when he worked here."

The groom blinked quickly.

"And ask if he would sponsor us for the Charity Ride," Rosie added, determined to get something good from the visit.

The groom's face lightened, and he laughed mockingly. "You're wasting your time on *that* score. You won't get a penny out of old Perryvale for charity," he said. "He hasn't got one to spare right now." The girls glanced at each other quickly, surprised at the groom's revelation. But he didn't notice, and continued. "And as for Billy Pyke, there's nothing to tell. He was sacked after he got caught letting horses out of one of our paddocks – simple."

"One of *your* paddocks?" Alice frowned. The groom nodded. "You mean, the horses that Billy let loose belonged to Mr Perryvale?"

"That's right," the groom sniffed, leaning on his broom.

"Did Mr Perryvale catch him doing it, then?" Charlie asked.

"No," the groom gave a satisfied smile. "*I* did."

"Oh, right," Rosie said, feeling confused. "But why would Billy let out Mr Perryvale's horses?"

The groom shrugged, looking like he'd said all he was interested in saying, and now he was getting bored. "I guess you'd have to ask Billy that. Anyway, if you want to speak to Mr Perryvale, there are business cards with his mobile number on in the tack room over there. Emma's inside, she'll show you."

"Okay, thanks." Mia slid out of the saddle, then gave her reins to Alice. She was just about to walk away, when the groom said something that made her stop in her tracks.

"I'm sure I recognise your ponies, by the way," he said, patting Wish. His tone was anything but friendly. "This one's so stunning, you can't miss her. They're stabled near Duck Lane, aren't they?"

Mia's blood ran cold. Before she knew it, a lie instinctively sprang from her. "Oh, no." She tried to smile lightly. "No, you must be thinking of another pony. We're the other side of the village."

The others nodded, but the groom raised one eyebrow, and gave a small chuckle before turning away with his broom. Over his shoulder, he said. "Well don't worry, I'll *be sure to* let Mr Perryvale know that you were here."

Mia's steps were stilted as she walked over

to the smart tack room. She wanted to take Wish and get as far away as possible. But as she shoved her hands into her pocket, she felt the hair she'd put in there earlier. It was Cracker's, and it gave Mia a sudden burst of courage. She knew they couldn't give up.

Mia pushed the door open and walked inside the bright room. Immediately she noticed the cobwebs, and the untidiness. It needed a good clear out. Emma was vigorously rubbing one of the smarter-looking saddles with some saddle soap and a sponge. She looked tired, but more approachable than the groom outside.

"Business cards are on the desk," she said with a brief smile.

"Thanks." Mia picked one up, and was about to go, when she noticed Emma stop polishing the saddle mid-rub, and glance at the open door. Then she stepped lightly towards it and gave it a little shove, so that it swung almost closed. Emma turned to Mia.

"Don't believe everything you hear about Billy, including from Max out there," Emma said quietly, nodding towards the door.

"I worked with Billy for ages, and what happened was completely out of character. Something never added up about those horses being let out. But Billy wouldn't breathe a word to anyone about it."

At that moment a phone rung outside. Emma jumped, like she'd had an electric shock, then hastily turned back to her tack. Mia heard Max talking in the yard, then the door swung open. Max bobbed his head round, and for a second looked suspicious.

"Long time to pick up a business card," he said, scowling at Mia. "And you should be concentrating on work, Emma. Boss left me in charge today, and he wants all this tack sparkling. Wants to get his money's worth out of you before you leave here for good. Look, I'm popping over to the Wollesley yard. They've just rung to let me know those imported polo ponies have arrived from Argentina. Apparently there are some seriously decent ones among them. Pricey, but the boss will persuade them to let him have some on credit. I reckon he needs to find a replacement for Stormchaser if we're going to win the Winter Cup again."

He gave Emma a thin smile, then disappeared.

Mia was confused. "What did he mean about Stormchaser?" she asked. "I thought he was Estoni's horse."

Emma shook her head then grabbed the bridle beside her, dunking the bit into a bucket of warm water. "Mr Perryvale bought him nearly a year ago from a yard in Argentina. Stormchaser was one in a long line of expensive horses that arrived here with massive reputations. The boss's plan was to put together the most expensive team of polo ponies in the country and Mr Perryvale wanted the glory for himself, so he'd always insist on riding the best ones. You know Nick Webb managed this place before he left to set up at the Abbey, right?"

Mia nodded.

"Well, Nick suggested to the boss that we get professional riders into the team, to get the best out of the ponies. But the boss wouldn't hear of it," Emma lowered her voice a notch. "You see, Mr Perryvale is a *seriously* untalented rider. These amazing horses would be here for a few months before he'd declare they were useless, because *he* couldn't control them. Next thing, the horses would be shipped out of the yard, goodness knows where. It drove Nick mad. But Mr Perryvale didn't care. All he cared about was that he looked good. If the horses didn't deliver, they were out of here. Anyway, Stormchaser was so wild, no one could get near him, let alone ride him. He was downright dangerous when he was here, and not just to ride. I guess that's why the boss decided to give Stormchaser to Nick when he left. It was his leaving gift."

"Wow, that was generous!" Mia frowned, thinking about how expensive Emma had said he'd been.

Emma gave a hollow laugh.

"Hardly," she said, with a grim smile. "Nick was the heart of this polo club. Mr Perryvale liked to think *he* was, but he knew deep down he was just the money man, and that Nick was the gifted horseman. That's why the boss was furious when Nick announced he was leaving. He knew the club would fail without Nick. So, Mr Perryvale wasn't being *generous* when he gave Stormchaser to Nick. He was hoping that Storm would injure every rider going. It was like the boss was giving Nick a clear message. Only, Mr Perryvale didn't anticipate Nick bringing an unknown Argentinean rider over to take on Storm. Nick traced Estoni, knowing that he was the rider who broke Storm in. Estoni knows the horse inside out, as well as being a talented polo player. Now Mr Perryvale has been left with egg on his face."

Emma was quiet for a second, then she continued, "Good luck to the Abbey team, I hope they win the Winter Cup, or at least do better than the Perryvale team. Although I don't think my boss feels quite the same way."

At that moment Rosie popped her head round the door. "Are you coming or what?" she asked Mia. "It's freezing hanging about out here. Your pony's got a fleecy exercise sheet wrapped round her rump, but I haven't!"

"Just coming," Mia said.

"Anyway, look, I've got to get on," Emma said, "it's my last day today, and the sooner I get this pile finished, the sooner I get to leave this sad old place. I've held on for as long as I can since Nick left, just for the polo ponies that are still here. But I can't hang on anymore. The boss is always in a bad mood and his liveries keep leaving now Nick's gone. This club will somehow scrape a team together for the Winter Cup – it'd be over Mr Perryvale's dead body that he'd let Nick win. But just so you know, Billy's a decent horseman, and a decent person, too."

"Thanks." Mia smiled at Emma, although she almost felt more confused than when she went in.

As Emma returned to her pile of tack with a sigh, Mia stepped back out into the icy blasts of December wind. A shivering Alice handed her Wish's reins. Suddenly an engine roared into life round the back of the stables. Phantom leaped forward and almost knocked Charlie flying. The girls turned to look, just as Max, in his Perryvale Polo Club jacket, skidded round the corner on a huge motorbike. He revved it loudly, spooking all the ponies. As the girls clung to their reins, the bike disappeared in a cloud of dirty fumes up the long drive. But not before Alice had noticed the cracked back number plate, which had a fragment of one corner missing.

◡ ◡ ◡ ◡

The girls rode home at a fast walk to keep the ponies warm, buzzing with their new information. They could hardly wait to get out to the hay barn and write it all down. Mia filled the others in on what Emma had told her, and they talked about the groom disappearing off on the motorbike with its splintered number plate.

They jogged the ponies down the track to Blackberry Farm, then they un-tacked and groomed their ponies, then chose the thickest outdoor rugs to put on them. Charlie put a duvet rug under Phantom's turnout rug, knowing how easily he got chilled, then the girls led their ponies to the paddock in headcollars.

When they got there, they slipped the headcollars off, giving their ponies plenty of pats and kisses. The ground in the paddock was still rutted and hard, but the ponies didn't do anything other than mooch over to the big piles of hay and munch. The piles were just in front of the open fronted field shelter, which protected them from the worst of the swirling winds.

Once the ponies were settled, the girls lugged their tack back to the tack room. Mia and Charlie wanted to have hot chocolates in the cottage kitchen, but Rosie had other ideas.

"I can't believe Max knew where our ponies live," she said with a shiver. "That seriously gave me the creeps. I reckon we should sit in the barn, so we can keep an eye on the ponies while they're out. I don't care how cold it is."

The others agreed and they hurried off to collect their hot drinks and a plate of piping hot toasted sandwiches from the kitchen. As soon as they were settled in the hay barn and wrapped up in blankets, with one eye on the paddock beyond, Mia hastily flipped open her notebook.

"Right, so now we know that Mr Perryvale's club is going down the drain," Rosie said, feeling her toes finally start to thaw. "His dream of having the best polo team around is totally failing."

"According to Emma," Mia added, "that's because Nick Webb left. Nick was the best horseman there, so without him, Mr Perryvale's stuffed."

"And to get his revenge, Mr Perryvale gave Nick Stormchaser, thinking he'd ruin the Abbey Polo Club before it even got going," Charlie added. "Only, he's ended up giving Nick's chances of winning the Winter Cup a huge boost instead."

"Exactly. Giving his rival the best polo pony around is hardly a good way to get revenge," Alice said, picking up Beanie and cuddling him to her for warmth. He licked the tip of her nose.

Mia looked up. "Okay, so let's get thinking…" she said. "What other way could Mr Perryvale get revenge *and* ruin the new polo club?"

Rosie, Alice and Charlie all looked at each other.

"We suspected that all those clues pointing to Billy were too obvious…" Charlie said, speaking fast as her mind whirred. "Like the Abbey biscuit wrapper being left at the scene, and a motorbike revving up each time."

"Especially as each of the places that were targeted," Alice added, "had signed the petition against the Abbey. And it was obvious, because it started from the top of the list. There was no guess work involved, all the clues were right there for anyone to find! Everything suggested that the Abbey was trying to get their own back on the local protestors."

"But now we know that Billy's not the only one with a motorbike," Rosie said, wiping a whipped cream moustache from the top of her lip. "Max has got one too, one with a more powerful engine."

"And with a number plate that's missing a corner," Alice pointed out, "it *has* to be the same one that was at Hope Farm last night."

"Exactly," Mia agreed. "If Mr Perryvale couldn't get revenge by giving Stormchaser to Nick, he had to find another way to ruin the new polo club. And turning everyone against the Abbey by setting up Billy was a pretty good start."

"And it's Mr Perryvale who's gone round telling everyone that Billy's done this before, remember," Alice added. "We wouldn't have even suspected Billy in the first place if he hadn't told us that. And Fran Hope said everyone in the village was talking about it. I bet Mr Perryvale's been spreading it round to everyone who'd listen, just like he did to us!"

"Only Mr Perryvale and Max made a mistake in letting out Cracker and Frostie from Fran's yard," Charlie said. "Hope Farm was next on the list, so that's where they targeted. *We* already knew that Nick wanted to rehome Cracker and Frostie, but Mr Perryvale and Max wouldn't have known that. There's no way Billy would have let out those horses, it wouldn't make sense. That shows this *must* have been a set up."

Mia's wrist ached from writing so quickly. She rubbed it as she sat back looking over her notes. But as she reread the clues, she began to frown.

"Hang on a sec…" she said slowly. "This doesn't quite add up."

"Really?" Rosie said, picking up another toastie from the plate. "How come?" She broke the sandwich in half and shared it with Beanie, who'd raised his soft muzzle and was sniffing the air hopefully.

"Well, if you think about it," Mia replied, "Nick's done a pretty good job of turning everyone against the Abbey all by himself, hasn't he? He's the one that's shut off all the rides there, not Mr Perryvale. If he hadn't done that, there wouldn't have been a petition in the first place."

The girls felt the old frustration flooding back as they realised that Mia was right. The case was still running rings around them.

Alice let out a huge sigh. "Everything still keeps leading us straight back to the Abbey," she said, tickling Pumpkin with a bit of hay. As the ginger cat pounced playfully, Alice looked up at the others. "We've got to get to the bottom of what's happening there first."

The next second Charlie's phone pinged with a text, making them all jump out of their skins.

"What does it say?" Alice asked, leaning over to get a better look.

"It's from Neve," Charlie said.

Just back from Xmas shopping to great news! Charity ride still on, in memory of Cracker. Abbey rides re-opened for it. See you at Abbey at 10! xx

"That's weird," Mia frowned. "I wonder what made Nick change his mind?"

"Who cares?" Charlie beamed. "This is our chance to get back inside the Abbey for a really good look around, and this time we don't even have to sneak our way in!"

Alice didn't feel anywhere near as thrilled. "Do you think it'll be okay, though?" she asked, looking anxious. "What about Mr Pyke?"

"There's no way Nick could let him loose during the Charity Ride, surely," Mia reasoned.

Rosie groaned. "Do I seriously have to squash back into that pudding costume again?"

"No, we shouldn't dress up," Mia said firmly. "We don't want to draw attention to ourselves, in case we need to go off the strict route. Turning up with bridles covered in sleigh bells or pink tinsel isn't going to help us creep about on any secret missions, is it?"

The girls looked at each other and broke into excited grins. The case may be the most complicated they'd taken on so far, but suddenly it felt like they'd just been given a key to a huge, locked door.

As they left the barn to move to the warmth of the kitchen, Phantom walked over to the field gate. He whickered silently to Charlie, who walked over to give him a pat. She felt his ears, which were chilly.

"I think I'm going to bring Phantom in," she decided, looking round. "And anyway, I don't think we should leave our ponies out while all this is going on, not while we're not here to keep an eye on them."

"I'm going to talk to Dad about putting a padlock on the yard gates, too," Rosie said, as they all picked up their headcollars and called their ponies over. "Especially after what that creepy groom said."

On the way back up to the stables, Mia, Charlie and Alice called their parents, to ask if they could stay over at Blackberry Farm until they could be sure that their ponies were safe.

But they all got a flat no.

"My mum says there's too much still to do at home before Christmas Day," Alice sighed.

"And my dad said I already spend so much time at the yard that he's almost forgotten what I look like," Charlie grumbled. She knew where she'd rather be – sleeping in Phantom's stable and keeping her precious horse safe. But she also knew that this was one battle she wouldn't be able to win.

"Well, I'll make sure the yard gate is locked tonight, and I can put Beanie on patrol," Rosie said, trying to make them feel better. They all looked at Beanie, who immediately rolled over, hoping he was about to get some fuss. Rosie shook her head.

The girls tried to encourage each other with smiles as they led their ponies back into the relative warmth of their stables. But they all knew that until the case was solved their ponies would never be one hundred percent safe.

Chapter Thirteen

THE Pony Detectives hadn't had time to make a plan for what they'd do at the Charity Ride the next morning, because they'd been too busy getting their ponies ready. As they were finishing off getting tacked up, Will wandered out to the yard.

"There's a bit in this morning's *Eastly Daily Press* about the Charity Ride today," he said, walking over to show the girls as they stood, ready to mount. Dancer immediately lunged for the paper, grabbing one corner with her long teeth and wagging her head up and down, shaking it all over the floor.

"Dancer, that is *so* not helpful!" Rosie puffed, yanking on her reins to get her mare's attention.

The page that Will had wanted them to see floated near to Scout's feet, and the grey pony lowered his muzzle enquiringly, while Phantom jinked sideways, away from it. Alice bent down to pick the paper up, then scanned the article quickly.

"Fran Hope must have contacted the *Daily Press*..." Alice said. "It's a reminder to everyone about the ride, and that it'll be meeting at the Abbey after all, just like previous years. It talks about not having to worry about any road work, because Nick Webb has set out a six mile route through the Abbey estate. It goes on to say that 'although relations between Nick Webb and the local equestrian community have been strained recently, Nick has gone out of his way to make sure that the Charity Ride goes ahead as planned. He'll even be working through the night to get a safe route marked out, because he said it was even more important now to raise funds for Hope Farm in memory of Cracker. The horse had been chosen by Nick as a new ride for some of the chukkas in the upcoming Winter Cup for his professional player, Estoni. This would take the pressure off the team's star polo pony, Stormchaser, who wouldn't be able to play in every chukka.' Then it says that

Fran Hope's really grateful, and hopes that the horsey community can put recent events behind them and pull together to support a really good cause. It's even got a reply from Mrs Maplethorp, who says that she'll encourage her Pony Clubbers to go if it leads to paths being reopened in the Abbey."

The girls looked at each other. "A *safe* route," Mia said slowly, as she tightened Wish's girth, and hopped into the saddle.

"How furious do you think Mr Perryvale's going to be, though?" Charlie asked, patting a prancing Phantom on his neck to calm him. She knew he wasn't being naughty, just keen to get going to keep warm. Charlie sat glued to her saddle. "Everything he's done recently has been with the aim of turning everyone against the Abbey polo club. Now that Nick's reopened the rides, do you think all the horsey people will have a change of heart?"

Rosie and Alice shrugged.

Mia folded the article and tucked it inside her coat pocket, next to Cracker's soft hair. Then the four girls and their ponies set off up the track to Duck Lane. As they walked, a fine, silver mist began to wend its way slowly through the trees and spill onto the lanes. The girls looked at each other, knowing what the mist had brought with it before. They rode on, with a growing sense of nervous anticipation.

᠊ ᠊ ᠊ ᠊

As the Pony Detectives approached the Abbey they saw big banners painted with 'Hope Farm Charity Ride' hung high across the entrance gates. They had wondered how many people were going to turn up, if any. Not only was the change of plan last minute, but they weren't sure how many riders still wanted to boycott the Abbey. But as they rode closer along the lane, they saw a large crowd already there and ambling about the arena. The girls looked around and heard Fran Hope's enormous infectious laugh before they saw her, which made them all smile. They stood in their stirrups and waved to Neve, who was on an excited Pirate.

Among the crowd was Mrs Maplethorp,

sitting on one of her ancient Highland ponies, and Mrs Greenfield, who was mounted on one of the riding school horses. Sophie was nearby, on Molly, with a bunch of the riding school regulars, plus Gracie and Debbie from Long Lane Livery.

The Pony Detectives were relieved, but not surprised. No matter what had happened at the polo club, everyone always turned out in force to support Fran Hope and the animals of Hope Farm. And this year the crowd looked bigger than ever. The girls were sure that was because news about what had happened to Cracker had spread.

As they walked through the main Abbey gates, towards the arena entrance, Alice caught a glimpse of the stables beyond. They weren't impressive and flashy, like Mr Perryvale's had once been, but they were neat and functional. Most of the doors were open and the polo ponies out, apart from a few, including the injured Thimble and Rumour, who were standing with their heads over the stable doors, watching the activity.

Alice could hear, even from where Scout was standing, the odd grumpy squeal, and then a wallop, as if back hooves were slamming against stable walls. She craned her neck round to see, and noticed a bay with a broad white face running his teeth up and down the metal bars of his stable. Stormchaser. Just his name made her spine tingle. The presence of so many horses was clearly winding him up to the point where he could almost explode. The way he was with other horses, let alone people, meant there was no way Estoni could take him on the Charity Ride, in among the crowd. Instead, Stormchaser was securely bolted within the confines of his stable, out of reach of everyone else.

The chatter of riders and the whinnies and shrill neighs of an assortment of horses and ponies soon filled the air. As everyone was ushered into the large arena, it turned into a riot of bright colours, with lots of riders in Christmassy dress. As they busily greeted each other, they were handed drinks of hot ginger punch from Nick and his grooms, in their distinctive bright red Abbey Polo Club jackets.

The hot, spicy drink burnt lines down the girls' throats, warming them up from the inside out.

Mia noticed that although Nick was smiling at everyone, he wasn't relaxed. Instead, his eyes were darting in every direction, like he was watching for something, only Mia had no idea what. The Pony Detectives looked round at the growing crowd. Then, they almost fell out of their saddles as they spotted India, grinning from ear to ear. She was sitting on top of Frostie, just outside the arena. He looked at ease in full polo tack, like he'd worn it hundreds of times before.

As India directed all the latest arrivals into the huge arena, Alice felt a lump in her throat, seeing Frostie's pricked ears and bright eyes. He looked excited to see the other ponies, and was clearly trusting of India's light touch. As the girls followed the other ponies and horses into the arena, Estoni, at the far end, on a rich chestnut, called over to India. India lightly touched her legs to Frostie's side and he moved smoothly from walk to canter. He cantered the length of the sand surface, and India turned him by gentle pressure of the reins on one side of his neck. She sat up in the saddle and Frostie immediately sank back onto his haunches and pulled himself up right next to Estoni.

"Frostie looks amazing!" Alice breathed, not knowing whether to laugh or cry.

"And he's one hundred percent done *that* before," Charlie said, looking confused. She turned to the others. "In fact, he looks like a ready-made polo pony."

"You know, I reckon Billy and India must have known that from the moment they first saw Frostie and Cracker," Mia said, almost to herself.

Alice nodded, as she leant forward to hug Scout, trying to keep herself warm. "And they must have told Nick as soon as they got back. I bet he called Fran right there and then."

The girls didn't have another chance to think about how Billy and India were able to tell Cracker and Frostie's polo potential, because at that moment Fran Hope's voice hollered down a megaphone, rising above all the noise.

"Welcome, everybody, to our annual Hope

Farm Charity Ride!" Fran smiled around at the huge, animated crowd, who cheered in reply. "Now, we're about to set off and I just have one thing to ask you all. The route we're riding today takes us along most of the pretty paths we all know and love so well, but I urge you to stay between the red markers at all times."

A murmur rippled around the crowd. Alice felt her stomach start to tighten with anxiety, hoping that Scout didn't get too overexcited amongst so many horses.

Fran cleared her throat and continued. "Nick Webb and his team have worked extra hard to painstakingly plan this route, and it is very important that you *all* stick to it, with no exceptions. Everybody clear?"

There were lots of cheers and general agreement.

"Then let's begin!" Fran cried above the noise. "Everybody follow India!"

The riders in the arena began to part, for India to ride her horse to the front. As she neared the Pony Detectives, Frostie looked over and whinnied. The girls called out hello to him, and India grinned, before patting him lightly on the neck.

"Good boy, Misty," Rosie overheard India tell him.

Rosie frowned. "Misty?"

India looked up sharply, bit her lip, then rode on quickly, disappearing into the crowd.

$$\cup\ \cup\ \cup\ \cup$$

"Let's stay near the back," Mia suggested. "That way we can break away when we get the chance."

The Pony Detectives let the bustling ponies and horses walk or trot on past them. Rosie leant forward along Dancer's neck and pretended to fiddle with her mare's bridle. Alice and Charlie struggled slightly with their ponies, who wanted to follow the crowd at once, while Wish stood placidly, taking everything in with her huge, soft eyes. Then they set off, too, and headed between the clearly marked starter flags. There were lots of different paths through the Abbey estate, and Charlie was excited to see which ones had been set up for the ride. She was hoping they'd be heading for the wide woodchip gallops, or the grass gallops, that were always watered and perfectly manicured. But instead, they were heading towards one of the winding paths that led through the woods. Charlie stood up in her stirrups and peered ahead at the red arrows that would keep them travelling in a strict direction. She would have loved to have been able to give Phantom a canter, but she knew that on this path they'd have to keep pretty much to a walk. Even so, right now the girls didn't really care. It was the first time they'd ridden off road and on a soft surface for ages, and their ponies had definitely perked up.

In the distance they could hear laughter and groups of riders breaking out into spirited Christmas carols. Normally Rosie would be the first to join in, singing tunelessly at the top of her voice. But today her mind was firmly focused on what lay ahead.

"Do you think Fran will still hand out mince pies at the end of the ride?" she asked.

"Rosie!" Mia cried. As Charlie and Alice

giggled, they heard a patter of hoof beats behind them. They turned in their saddles and saw Archie trotting his little grey, Rascal, to catch up with the ride. Archie gave them a small, shy smile. But he jogged his pony past them without pausing for any conversation. As Archie went, the girls heard Billy call out from the crowd of riders ahead.

"Make sure everyone stays on course, Archie."

The girls caught sight of Billy's expression under his helmet, before he turned back round. He looked as anxious as Nick had done in the arena. Archie nodded, then caught up with the group of riders on the path ahead.

Suddenly, an echoing shot cracked out in the far distance. Phantom jumped forward, ears back and Charlie felt his heart skip, beneath her legs. She sat quietly and kept her reins soft until her horse calmed again.

Scout pricked his ears and dodged sideways. Alice, who was looking in the other direction, suddenly found herself ditched out of the saddle. She landed with a thud on her bottom, and rolled backwards while Scout rushed forward and bumped into Dancer.

Alice picked herself up. Putting a brave face on it, she rubbed her hip quickly and dusted down her brown jods, before collecting Scout. Her pony nudged her apologetically.

"That's all right, Scout," she said, rubbing his forehead, "I don't blame you for being scared, not after last time."

"I can't believe Mr Pyke's got his gun out again today!" Charlie tutted. "How crazy is that?"

"Come on, we'd better trot to catch up with the others," Rosie said.

"Although," Mia said, narrowing her eyes, "maybe Alice's tumble has given us the perfect opportunity to get off this track. We can look for a reason why Nick might have shut off the rides, and why they aren't safe, while everyone's preoccupied. Come on, let's go. And keep your eyes open!"

The girls had a quick check around them. Ahead, the tail end of the ride was disappearing, and the voices and carols were fading. There was no one behind them. Mr Pyke was miles away, if the gun shot was anything to go by. With hearts beating fast, they turned their ponies away from the red flags.

Chapter Fourteen

THE four ponies stepped quietly along a leaf-strewn path. It was a perfect place for a canter, and at the head of the group, Charlie was about to let Phantom stride forward, when she suddenly pulled him to the left. Phantom snorted, lifting his nose in the air at the unusual, hard yank on the reins.

"Careful where you walk," Charlie said over her shoulder to the others, turning Phantom and patting his neck. "It looks like there's some kind of hole down there."

The girls looked down at the ground, where there was a ruffle in the grass, like it had been disturbed. The ground dipped and some of the mossy covering was missing. Mia wrinkled her nose.

Charlie rode on carefully ahead. "There's another one here, and up there."

Rosie slipped out of the saddle and knelt

down next to one of them. Dancer immediately decided to help her check the hole, and shoved her muzzle almost into it. Rosie pushed Dancer's nose out of the way, then continued to puzzle at the ground. By the side of the path she noticed a small mound of earth.

"These holes looks like they've been dug out on purpose." Rosie said, standing back up and leaning against Dancer, soaking up some of her warmth.

"That's so dangerous," Alice shook her head. "Why would anyone do that on a path that horses use all the time?"

As the girls stood, the atmosphere around them changed. A chill dampness closed in. An uneasy silence had descended; there was no birdsong, nothing. The silver mist was beginning to drift through the trees again. Rosie half wished she was in the big bunch of other riders, so that if this mist got worse they'd all be in it together, rather than wandering about in a small group

"We'd better keep moving, come on," Mia shivered.

Rosie stayed on the ground as they carried on, walking Dancer at the front and keeping her eyes peeled for any more holes. If one of the ponies put their hooves down it, they could easily sprain a fetlock, if not worse. Rosie stopped dead, her breath coming short as the thought occurred to her that the holes could be significant.

"Hang on! This is it!" Rosie squeaked. "I bet this was how Thimble and Rumour got injured! Their riders might *not* have been careless when they were exercising them!"

Mia nodded. It made sense. "Someone could have tried to injure the Abbey polo ponies *on purpose*."

The girls walked in silence for a second, trying to take in what that meant.

"This could be why Nick made sure that the Charity Ride sticks so strictly to that red route," Charlie suggested. "It said in the newspaper that he'd been up all night checking it and putting up the markers, remember?"

"He *knew* that parts of the normal rides through the Abbey weren't safe," Mia said, starting to feel a tingle of adrenalin as the mysteries suddenly began to crystallise in her mind.

"Do you reckon that's what Archie meant," Rosie gasped, "when he said it wasn't safe to ride around the Abbey?"

"He might not have been talking about Mr Pyke and his gun after all," Alice said, as realisation struck her like a thunderbolt. "He might have meant the paths weren't safe for *any* horses, so they couldn't let anyone in here. Maybe that's why they blocked up all the entrances!"

"And why the ponies were being exercised around the lanes," Mia added, "rather than in the estate!"

"Fair enough," Rosie frowned, "but why didn't Nick just *say* that's why he closed the rides? I mean, everyone would've understood if he'd done it to keep horses safe."

Charlie nodded. "Whatever his reason, it doesn't help us get any closer to finding out why anyone would deliberately try to hurt a horse, and especially like this." She felt a cold sweat break out. She'd wanted to canter

Phantom along that path. Her fine limbed horse was lucky to still be walking on all four legs... Charlie put the thought from her mind, and focused on what they already knew – that someone recently had been putting horses' lives at risk without a care.

"Emma said something..." Mia said, concentrating hard as she recalled their conversation. "Oh yes, for Mr Perryvale, horses are just machines to get him glory. If they don't do that, they're chucked out. He doesn't care about them. All he cares about is making himself look good. Oh, and winning the Winter Cup..."

"And right now," Rosie said, her breathing coming fast, "Nick's likely to beat him, as long as he has Stormchaser in his team."

"Stormchaser..." Mia gasped. "Maybe he's the key to this! Mr Perryvale gave him to Nick hoping he'd injure the riders and ruin the team before it had even got started. But instead the horse Mr Perryvale gave away became the Abbey's star. So what does Mr Perryvale try next? First, he tries to ruin the club's reputation, by making out that Billy is responsible for riding round on his motorbike letting out horses. But what if that wasn't the only way Mr Perryvale was trying to ruin the Abbey? What if he dug holes in this land, wanting to injure Nick's team of horses...?"

"If that really is the case, it sounds like Mr Perryvale will stop at nothing to see Nick Webb fail," Charlie said, shaking her head.

"And there was something else Emma said..." Mia wracked her brains. Suddenly her face dropped. "She said that Mr Perryvale would let Nick beat him in the Winter Cup *over his dead body*. He's really serious about not being beaten."

"But while the Abbey is still up and running, and while they still have Stormchaser on their team, they've still got a good chance of lifting the Cup," Alice said, her mind racing.

"So what if *Stormchaser's* been Mr Perryvale's target all along," Rosie said, starting to panic, "with all these holes in the gallops? What if it's over Stormchaser's dead body...? They didn't care about Cracker dying when Max let him out of Hope Farm. They might not stop there!"

While they'd been talking, the girls had been looking at the holes in the ground. When they looked up, they realised the mist had rolled in swiftly. Now it surrounded them with its icy chill. They couldn't hear a sound from the charity riders, who had moved on far into the distance. The girls' vision along the path through the woods was getting patchy, and they didn't have a clue who was around.

"So far, its seems like Mr Perryvale and Max normally operate at night," Mia said, her blood running cold.

"Unless there's an opportunity during the *day*," Charlie shivered, "when everyone else is occupied with a big Charity Ride..."

"And the mist is around to give them cover..." Alice added, as goosebumps rose all over her.

"We need to get to the stables," Rosie squeaked. "Fast!"

The girls started to jog their ponies, keeping a lookout for holes while they headed through the ever-thickening mist. The grey outline of the arena emerged in front of them through the haze. The stables were to the left of the arena and most of the stable doors were open. As the ponies' metallic shoes clopped on the concrete leading up to the stables, Thimble and Rumour bobbed to their doors. But the girls were aware of one thing: silence. Alice felt her heart begin to thump harder. Stormchaser was never silent, even in his stable. And that could only mean one thing...

As they rode through the gloom, they all gasped at the same moment. Stormchaser's stable door hung wide open.

Then they heard what sounded like someone walking with a limp. The girls looked at each other, willing their ponies to stay quiet. There was a grunt, as someone emerged from the woodland at the other side of the entrance to the drive. A car door clicked open, then clunked shut. An engine purred into life and the mist cleared momentarily, revealing a Range Rover that was parked right across the Abbey's exit. Its driver reversed, straightening up, then revved hard before accelerating past the girls and their ponies, scattering pebbles from the drive in its wake. The driver didn't even look left or right. He didn't see them standing by the entrance to the stable block. He leant forward, going hell for leather to get out of the estate.

As the Range Rover accelerated past them, the girls saw the insignia on the side of the door – it was for Perryvale's Polo Club.

∪ ∪ ∪ ∪

The Pony Detectives didn't waste a second. As soon as the Range Rover was out of sight they jogged their ponies over to where Mr Perryvale's car had been.

Alice felt all the hairs on the back of her neck stand up. "Look at those footprints!" she squeaked.

The others stared as she'd pointed to an impression left on the frosted drive. One foot, the left, was a full print. But the right was just of the front of a boot.

"Fran said he'd had a bad accident," Rosie remembered with a rush, "and that he couldn't walk very well. Maybe his limp explains the odd print!"

"The same one that we saw by the common land!" Charlie said. "*He* must have been the one who dumped Cracker and Frostie there! I bet that's the way he gets rid of his *useless* polo ponies!"

"I bet Max staked out the land first!" Rosie gasped. "*That's* how he knew about our ponies!"

"And if those two horses were at Perryvale," Alice squealed, "India and Billy would've known them. They knew they were trained to play polo!"

"All that's important, guys, but right now we have to concentrate on what's happened to Stormchaser," Mia said, feeling slightly queasy at the thought. She knew they had no time to lose.

"Mia's right," Alice agreed, scouring the ground from Scout's back. "We need to think. If Mr Perryvale blocked the path out of the estate with his Range Rover, then let Stormchaser out of his stable, where would the horse be most likely to go? Where would Mr Perryvale try to direct him, wanting the maximum damage to happen to him?"

The girls looked around them, but they

couldn't see far in the mist. Charlie felt her heart skip a beat.

"Well, there's only one place that's guaranteed to end in disaster," she said, feeling her stomach churn. "Think about it, I bet Stormchaser exploded straight out of the stables. If the main path out of the estate was blocked by Mr Perryvale's Range Rover, he'd have galloped straight ahead and shot straight into these woods. I reckon he'll have headed for the woodland path that lies alongside Mr Perryvale's land."

"The one our ponies bolted up the other day!" Mia gulped.

"Exactly," Charlie said grimly. "And if he's scared Stormchaser into a flat out gallop, he'll follow that path right to the other end of the estate. The trees are so dense that he wouldn't even think of ducking off in any other direction..."

"... and he'll fly straight into that cattle grid." Alice felt sick as she pictured the scene.

"We *have* to head him off," Mia said urgently. "But we can't just chase him, we'll make him go faster. We'll have to go out onto the estate paddocks and head straight across them. We'll beat him to the cattle grid that way, because the path he'll be on curves right round and it's much longer. Come on!"

Mia didn't wait for an answer. She pressed her legs to Wish's sides. Her pony flickered her ears back, leaping forward and putting her trust fully in her rider. The mist was so thick that they could hardly see in front of them, but Mia knew her way past the stable block and up onto a long grassy expanse. It ran alongside the edge of the woods, but it wasn't a path. She was just praying that that meant Mr Perryvale hadn't dug any holes in it.

The four girls started off riding alongside each other, but Phantom and Wish soon began to draw ahead. While they were cantering through the swirling mist, Charlie wracked her brain about how they could possibly stop Stormchaser from careering straight over the cattle grid. It was straight on his line, and if they couldn't stop him, he'd gallop full speed into it. He wouldn't have a rider to steady him, or help lift him up into the air. He wouldn't know to jump it, like Phantom had. Instead his hooves would plunge straight through the metal grid. It came to her in a sudden flash – they only had one choice. And that was to play him at his own game – to act like it was a game of polo. One of their four ponies would have to block Stormchaser's path. And the only pony solid enough to even begin to do that, was Dancer.

Charlie glanced behind her. They wouldn't have much time to put her plan into place. She glimpsed Rosie standing up in her stirrups, bending low over Dancer's neck, urging her mare on. Dancer poked out her nose, responding to Rosie and stretching out further, her nostrils flaring as her legs pumped. Rosie's face was a pale mask of determination as she tried to get her mare going as fast as she could.

Just as Dancer was starting to slow, the far end of the estate came into sight. The wooded path that they thought Stormchaser was on followed the edge of the estate, and as fast as the polo pony may be galloping, the Pony Detectives knew they'd still beat him to the grid.

Charlie was first to pull up. Phantom was still full of running, and Charlie had to fight for a second to slow him to a walk. His breath plumed heavily and he continued bouncing. Charlie had to hold onto him tightly while the others pulled up around her.

Dancer was at the back, puffing, her neck dark with sweat.

"So what do we do now?" Rosie gulped, trying to get in air.

"Stormchaser will come charging out of the woods, straight for this grid, just like Phantom did," Charlie said, out of breath too. "This mist will hide it from his view. We'll have to try to guide Storm off his line, like we've seen other riders try to in the arena, before he gets here."

Alice shook her head. "But we've never seen another polo pony manage that in the arena!" she pointed out, thinking that Scout would be tiny and powerless next to Stormchaser's heavy bulk. "What happens if we can't turn him?"

"Rosie, I think Dancer will have to block his path," Charlie said grimly. "She's the sturdiest of all our ponies. If he sees Dancer standing side on, by the cattle grid, he might just duck away in the last stride."

"You know he won't!" Rosie squealed. "Barging other ponies out of the way is Stormchaser's trademark move in the polo arena – the other ponies are terrified of him! I can't ask Dancer to do that!"

"If you don't," Charlie said, trying to stay calm, "Stormchaser will break his legs, right here in front of us! He could come galloping out at any moment - we've got to do something and we haven't got time to argue! I'm going to try to ride alongside him, Mia, I'll need you for that too. We'll try to turn him before he gets to you, Rosie, but you need to come and stand here, now! Alice, you and Scout stand between Rosie, and me and Mia. If me and Mia can't turn Stormchaser from his path, it'll be down to you to try to shift him before he reaches Dancer!"

Charlie ignored the terror on Rosie and Alice's faces, she had to. She turned Phantom, and cantered him away into the mist. Mia, looking uncertain of their plan, said good luck to Rosie before cantering Wish after Phantom.

Rosie trembled all over as she realised the huge responsibility Charlie had given her and her cobby mare, but they didn't have any choice if they were to have the slightest chance of saving Stormchaser. She felt terrified, but she'd just have to pray that Charlie's plan worked from the start. Then Charlie and Mia would have diverted Storm to safety by the time he reached the grid. Rosie pushed Dancer into position on the dirt track, and sat there, shaking.

Alice turned in the saddle. "Will you be okay?" She asked, looking anxious.

Rosie nodded, trying to look confident, even if she didn't feel it. Alice took a deep, frosty breath and trotted Scout into position, just beyond the mist. Suddenly Rosie was all alone with Dancer, in their small, silent pocket of visibility.

◡ ◡ ◡ ◡

Charlie and Mia cantered their ponies nearer to the exit from the woods. Charlie's heart felt like it might burst out of her chest. She stood in the hushed silence, barely able to see the exit, feeling the freezing mist close in around her. Phantom wouldn't stand still. He danced beneath Charlie, swirling and wanting to be off. She could tell that his nerves were getting seriously on edge, as the seconds ticked by. Then suddenly, another distant gunshot rang out, echoing around the woods and spooking the ponies.

"No!" Charlie cursed under her breath as Phantom's head came up and he bounded under her. Charlie grabbed at her reins, and it was all she could do to turn Phantom back towards the woods, when suddenly, bursting out of a gap in the trees at full flight, powered a thundering Stormchaser. His nostrils were flaring as he snorted furiously, the whites of his eyes wild.

The bay horse's bulk was low to the ground, his body like a ball of taut muscle. Phantom wheeled round, spinning away from him and almost throwing Charlie from the saddle. Mia closed her legs around Wish, and the obedient mare leapt forward to race alongside Stormchaser. Charlie finally managed to turn Phantom back. She sat in her saddle and drove her horse on, pushing with her hands on the reins until she and Mia were both flat out to the right of Storm.

Charlie urged her black horse on, edging Phantom in front of Storm and trying to angle into Storm's bulky shoulders, to try and turn him. Mia took Charlie's lead, angling Wish towards Storm, too. But Storm put his ears back, stretched out his muzzle, wrinkling his nostrils. As Charlie opened her rein to steer Storm, the bay horse drew back his lips and flashed his teeth towards Phantom's neck. Charlie tried desperately to get Phantom to keep his position, but her horse ducked away from Storm's wild aggression. Wish baulked sideways in the same stride as Phantom and in an instant Charlie knew that their first chance was gone. Phantom and Wish had fallen behind Storm, and to give chase now would only make the polo pony race faster. They began to slow down, panting for breath. Stormchaser's fate was now in Alice and Rosie's hands.

Rosie sat on Dancer, her teeth chattering uncontrollably between her blue lips. In the distance, behind her, she could hear the shouts, laughter and songs of the Charity Ride breaking through the silence. The riders, and Nick and his staff, had no idea what was going on under the blanket of mist which had descended on the Abbey grounds. Rosie felt her whole body tremble. She closed her eyes for a second, biting her lip.

"We can do this, Dancer," she whispered, leaning down to hug her mare's warm neck. Dancer had her ears back, and her head up nervously.

"Are you okay?" Alice called over from where she was standing, just merging into the mist. Rosie opened her mouth to shout back, "Of course not," but she never got the chance. All of a sudden, Alice was distracted, and turned round as Scout's head shot up and he began to bounce beneath her. Rosie peered through the mist, but she heard him before she saw him – the unmistakable rhythm of thundering hooves. She felt her legs go weak, even though she was sitting on Dancer. Her mare suddenly planted herself in fear, refusing to budge, her chunky legs splayed and her eyes goggling. Rosie stared, transfixed, as in front of her, Scout began to canter steadily towards Dancer. Then, in the next instant, the heavy figure of Stormchaser burst through the silver haze, in full flight, his hooves pounding the earth.

Rosie watched, aghast, as Alice tried desperately to push the bull-like bay off his course. She managed to steer him away a fraction, and as Stormchaser snaked his head angrily, he slowed ever so slightly. But Alice couldn't shift him enough. By the time Scout was outrun, the polo pony was still careering headlong for the cattle grid. All that stood between Storm and the death trap was Rosie and Dancer. But stopping Stormchaser looked as impossible as stopping a high speed train.

"Be brave, Dancer," Rosie whispered, trying desperately not to close her eyes, "we're in this together!"

Rosie could feel that Dancer was still frozen to the spot. She gulped, and did what Charlie had told her, waiting for as long as she dared. Then, at the very last second, as Stormchaser thundered towards her, Rosie realised that there was no way Dancer could bodily stop Stormchaser at that speed, and survive. Rosie suddenly changed the plan, and booted Dancer into life. For half a breath, Dancer didn't respond, too terrified to move.

"Move!" Rosie yelled, desperately. Then her stocky mare sprung forward, out of Storm's path. But Dancer was a heartbeat too late to get completely out of his way and Stormchaser careered into her hind quarters. The momentum sent him tumbling to the earth and spun Dancer round, taking her off her hooves and sending both the mare and Rosie thudding to the ground.

"Rosie, no!"

Rosie heard Alice's voice cry out as she covered her head, skidding across the hard drive, just narrowly avoiding Dancer's bulk as her mare almost rolled over, her legs straight in the air. Rosie twisted from where she lay, in time to see Storm skidding across the hard ground on his side. He came to a rest just over the cattle grid. Rosie moved to sit up, but she felt dizzy and dropped back to the ground. Before she knew it Alice was by her side.

"Are you okay, Rosie?"

Rosie managed a nod, but she was winded, and couldn't speak. As Dancer heaved herself back upright, she gave herself a shake. Dancer took three wobbly steps towards her owner, then stopped. Rosie could see blood beading and trickling from grazes on her mare's knee and shoulder, her muzzle and above her eye. Rosie felt panic rise in her chest, then Dancer lowered her head gingerly and began to nibble the grass. Rosie had never felt happier to see Dancer eating, and limped over to give her brave mare the biggest hug she could manage.

Charlie and Mia had caught up and had flung themselves out of their saddles. The pair of them stood in silent disbelief for a split second, taking in the scene that greeted them.

Stormchaser let out a long groan, followed by a snort. He looked winded, and momentarily stunned. Then he jerked his head up. One front leg, then the other, slipped between the metal bars as he stretched them out to stand.

For a moment, everyone was still. Then Stormchaser seemed to realise that he was trapped. Like an explosion, the bull-like bay suddenly burst into life. He thrashed in an attempt to get up. It was like he couldn't understand how he could kick his back legs, but not his front legs. And all his efforts did was trap his front legs even more and set him off into another frenzied attempt to stand.

The Pony Detectives were paralysed by the sight of the wild, crazed horse in front of them, his billowing breath heavy and stressed. There was no way they could safely get near him. The ear-splitting screech of metal shoes on the iron bars shattered the silence as the bay horse struggled furiously again, but in vain. He came to another uneasy, abrupt halt, his sides heaving.

Stormchaser looked around desperately, wildly, towards the group of girls and their ponies. He locked eyes with Mia, and in the stillness that followed, he let out a piercing neigh. Mia felt as if he had spoken straight to her, crying out in a direct, urgent appeal for help.

She responded instinctively. In an instant, Mia put her own fear to one side and walked quickly to where Storm was lying. She had to rescue him. Without thinking, she dropped on her knees next to the grid. She took hold of his head as firmly as she could, and held him close to her to try and secure him. The bay horse paused for a moment. Lying there, his massive bulk shaking and his nostrils flared red, he looked once more at Mia. His head was broad and Mia could feel his heavy skull beneath his silky, hot skin. His breath was coming in sharp billows.

For the briefest moment Storm was still. Mia felt his head shift ever so slightly. He fixed her with his deep, black eye, drawing her in. She felt a tingling sensation, like she was being examined by a fierce intelligence. Despite his obvious pain, there was pride and majesty staring back at Mia, and momentarily, she felt privileged to be allowed to get so close to such a raw force.

In that second, it was as if Stormchaser was thanking her for responding to his call.

Then the strange connection melted away. Storm attempted to stand again. He panicked, setting off another round of metallic clashes. Mia closed her eyes and held on for dear life, as she was thrown around by the almighty power of the horse beside her. It was all she could think of to do, to try and keep him as still as possible by anchoring his head. That way the damage to his legs might be less devastating.

She could hear the warning cries of her friends behind her, but Mia clung on, desperate to help the powerful horse, feeling the pulse thudding in his neck. She couldn't abandon him now. But suddenly, she sensed Storm fall into an uneasy calm.

"Someone's coming!"

Mia heard Alice cry out, but she didn't dare let Stormchaser go. And, as he heard running footsteps, and distant cries somewhere behind him, he began once more to try to stand, and to panic.

Mia glanced round, and her heart froze.

Mr Pyke was racing through the mist towards them, his gun slung over his arm. She watched as he assessed the situation in a heartbeat, and took his gun with the other hand. Mia gulped for breath, and felt a warm tear roll down her cheek, tensing as Stormchaser began to thrash around once more. She turned back towards Storm, tightly closing her eyes. Mia wanted nothing more than to shield the magnificent horse from the bullet that she felt sure would follow. But as his fight rose again she was unable to think of anything other than holding Storm still. She didn't yet know if his legs had been broken in the fall, or in the flailing around once he was down, but it was looking less and less likely that he could get out of this unhurt. Mia gripped Storm as he wildly battled to stand once more, then just as suddenly, he appeared to calm again, groaning deep within his chest.

There was a pause. The gunshot hadn't rung out as Mia had expected, and she dared to look up. She saw the gun on the grass by the edge of the grid. Mia immediately felt her heart start to find a rhythm again. She wanted to sob with relief, but she held it in, not wanting to scare Storm. She watched, her breath unsteady as Mr Pyke quickly weighed up the situation. He didn't flinch, or give anything away, and immediately got on to his radio.

"Nick, get the vet quickly, up by the cattle grid," he barked. "And the fire brigade, there's a horse stuck in the cattle grid." There was a pause. "It's Storm."

Then he turned to Mia. She braced herself, but, to her surprise, she had no need to.

"I would ask what on earth you four girls are doing up here on your own, when we told everyone to stick to the red flag route," Mr Pyke said in a gentle voice, "but for now, I think we should focus on what's happening here. Have you got any idea how Storm got out of his stable?"

"We think we might," Alice said cautiously, feeling relieved that Mr Pyke wasn't furious. She didn't want to bring Scout any closer, so she spoke from where she stood, a little distance away. Even so, she could see Mr Pyke's anxious expression, and she decided to be honest about what they'd been up to. "We... we wanted to find out why it was so unsafe to ride in the Abbey land. So, we ducked away from the ride at the first chance. We headed towards the stables and we'd nearly got there when we heard someone coming out of the woods, opposite. Then we saw Mr Perryvale limp back over to his Range Rover and drive off."

"Storm's door was already open by then," Charlie added, one hand still resting on Phantom's neck, "and he was gone."

Mr Pyke's face flashed with a silent anger, and his cheeks flushed a deep red. "That man's a disgrace to the horse world," he spat out. Storm started to move again. Mr Pyke helped Mia to hold him as still as they could. Only this time, Mia noticed, Storm's fight had lessened, like the fire inside him was slowly fading.

In the uneasy silence that followed, Charlie said in a whisper, "We found some holes dug into the ground in the woods. Did Mr Perryvale do that, too? To try and injure your polo team?"

Mr Pyke laughed mirthlessly. "That's just the start of it. We found barbed wire half buried into the gallops, too. He even put up a crop scarer on his field on the edge of our best training ride."

"What's a crop scarer?" Alice asked, leaning against Scout for warmth.

"It sounds like a gun," Mr Pyke explained. "It goes off randomly to scare birds away. Only trouble is, it spooks horses. It's on Mr Perryvale's land, so there was nothing we could do, but he put it right next to our woodland gallops. That's why we shut off all the rides, we had no choice until we could work out what to do about it, what was safe and what wasn't."

Charlie suddenly felt her own cheeks flush red, and she bit her lip. "We thought that was you shooting your gun."

Mr Pyke's eyes widened. "Why would you think I'd do anything so dangerous?"

Rosie, still feeling pretty dazed from her fall, piped up. "Er, because you carry a gun?"

"For pheasant shooting, away from horses." Mr Pyke muttered. "I wouldn't take pot shots at horses, or *riders*."

The four girls exchanged a quick, guilty look.

"Mr Perryvale has been determined to ruin Nick," Mr Pyke said, "ever since he walked out."

"So why *did* Nick leave?" Charlie asked, as Phantom began to get restless. She moved him further away, so he didn't unsettle Storm.

"Nick confronted Mr Perryvale about all the top horses that kept disappearing after they'd been ruined," Mr Pyke told them, keeping an eye on Storm as he spoke. "Mr Perryvale muttered about them being rehomed, but no one ever heard about any new owners. Billy was as suspicious as Nick about what had happened to them, and he was determined to find out. He hung back one evening and overheard Mr Perryvale talking to Max, asking him to *dump* another couple. Well, Billy tried to smuggle them out first to save them, but Max caught him. Max bragged to Billy about what he did for Mr Perryvale. He used to take them quite a distance away, so no one got suspicious. But they must have got lazy, because the last two were dumped on your doorstep. Anyway, Mr Perryvale was furious with Billy for interfering. He was sacked on the spot, and Mr

Perryvale kicked me and Archie out too. That was the final straw for Nick. He took on the Abbey and he offered us jobs as soon as it was up and running."

Mia carried on stroking Storm's forelock, as everything started to fall into place, including Mr Perryvale dumping Cracker and Frostie. But one thing didn't make sense. "So, why didn't you say anything when you realised that the tracks in here were being sabotaged?"

Mr Pyke glanced at Storm. His flanks were still heaving, his restfulness temporary and uneasy. "Well, we weren't sure who was behind it all to begin with," Mr Pyke confessed. "And even when Nick began to suspect Mr Perryvale, we had no proof. Nick was just starting to realise the depths that Mr Perryvale could sink to, so he was worried about making things even worse for his horses. But it looks like Mr Perryvale's pretty much done his worst, and achieved what he set out to do. Storm's chances in the Winter Cup are over..."

Mr Pyke didn't look at the girls. Instead he cleared his throat and fell silent. As Mia felt the warmth of Storm seeping through her coat, she couldn't help wondering if it was just Storm's chance of playing in the Winter Cup that had ended.

The sound of an engine broke through the mist. It grew louder, and a silver estate car suddenly appeared, approaching from the other side of the cattle grid. As the car braked, Nick and Estoni leapt out. A tall man carrying a leather bag climbed out after them – the vet, Mia supposed. Just behind, flashing lights glowed in the mist. The fire engine had arrived.

At the new disturbance, Storm broke out into a fresh, vigorous attempt to stand. Within seconds the tall man was approaching, a long needle in his hand. Without a moment's hesitation he knelt by Storm's side. As Storm paused for a second, the man expertly administered an injection. Storm snorted and shook his head, but the man held on firmly.

Before Mia had even counted to three, Storm's head grew heavy in her arms. She felt tears well in her eyes and tumble down her cheeks. She looked up at the others desperately.

"I'll take over from here," Estoni said gently, crouching next to Mia, his eyes fixed on his favourite polo pony. Mia didn't want to let go, but she knew it was important for Estoni to hold his horse. She dropped one kiss onto Stormchaser's closing eyelid, then slid out to let Estoni hold him. He cradled the bay horse's head, and whispered softly into his ear.

Mia felt stiff and bruised as she stood up and watched Nick place a rug over Stormchaser's prone, still body. The girls stood next to their ponies, unable to find any words. They heard Fran's voice, and looked up to see the Charity Ride a short distance ahead of them, shocked by what they had stumbled across. Mr Pyke quickly walked towards the group, ushering them back down to the arena. They disappeared once more into the mist, and their voices faded.

Nick turned to the Pony Detectives. "You'd better get your ponies back and warmed up," he said wearily, as the firemen got began to fetch their metal cutters and winches from the engine. "We can take everything from here."

The girls nodded. Then Nick caught sight of

Rosie's pale face and Dancer's clotted injuries and his eyes opened wide.

"What on earth happened here?"

Charlie took a deep, jagged breath, and started to explain.

Chapter Fifteen

THE Pony Detectives woke up together on Christmas Eve, in Rosie's bedroom. The silvery mist had finally rolled away and the sun had come out and thawed the frozen landscape. The events of the day before already seemed completely unreal to all the girls.

When Nick had found out exactly how the girls had been involved with trying to save Storm, he'd had his vet check Dancer thoroughly. All her wounds had been cleaned out and dressed, and the vet had declared her fit enough to travel. Nick had loaned all the ponies rugs and one of the grooms had dropped them back at Blackberry Farm in Nick's own horsebox.

Despite their parents' protests, the girls had refused point blank to go home, and had stayed the night at Blackberry Farm, giving their ponies lots of fuss and extra treats. Dancer even had extra hay in her haynet, and the four friends had done a special midnight check to make sure they'd got over their ordeal. Dancer was loving all the extra fuss, and drooped her head every time one of them walked past, just in case another treat might come her way.

Dancer was stiff when Rosie turned her out in the morning. The strawberry roan mare was walking gingerly, but Rosie knew after the vet check that it was nothing that some quiet walking on a lead rope around the lanes over the rest of the Christmas holidays couldn't cure.

"I think someone ought to tell Dancer that," Charlie smiled, as Dancer looked round for sympathy. Rosie gave her pony a huge hug; she couldn't have been more proud of Dancer for being so monumentally brave. Dancer gave her a droopy headed look, then nudged her pocket.

"Dancer, this can't go on forever you know," Rosie smiled, finding a slightly limp carrot in her jacket and holding it out for her mare. Dancer chomped it contentedly, before hobbling off to join the others at the hay piles.

The girls spent the rest of the day in a bit of a daze. They sat in Rosie's toasty kitchen until the afternoon sun dipped behind the trees, and it grew dark, busily wrapping the presents they had bought and stashed in the tack room for their ponies. The girls had got so cold the day before, partly from shock, that it had taken them ages to finally warm up, so Mrs Honeycott made sure they had a constant supply of hot chocolate.

"I still feel a bit weird, actually," Rosie said as she put down the Sellotape. "I'd better have another chocolate from the tree to boost my sugar levels."

"I don't think it'll just be Dancer who milks this for ages, do you?" Alice winked at Mia.

As they wrapped, the friends went back over what had happened the day before. With Mia's photos of the boot print and tyre tracks that were left when Cracker and Frostie were dumped, not to mention the fragment of the number plate from Max's bike, Nick had been sure that the police would agree to investigate

Mr Perryvale, and his head lad. And he was hopeful that Billy's name would be completely cleared in the process.

"I wonder if the investigation will be finished before the Winter Cup," Rosie said.

"I hope so," Charlie replied, with a slight frown. "But even if it's not, I don't reckon the Perryvale team would *dare* turn up to compete. They'd get booed out of the arena!"

"Especially after what happened to Stormchaser..." Alice choked, tears suddenly filling her eyes without warning.

"Either way," Rosie said quickly, trying to cheer things up before everyone got upset, "we'll need to get some sleep after everything that's happened in the past few weeks. Or we'll snore our way through the whole thing!"

"No snoring allowed," Mia said, forcing a bright smile. "Nick promised us the best seats in the house – remember?"

After the final present was wrapped, the girls took them out to the stables and carefully slid them into the stockings hanging on the front of the stable doors. Then they brought their ponies in and spent ages pampering them.

"They were all seriously brave yesterday," Charlie said, still thrilled by Phantom almost matching strides with the most awesome polo pony ever.

"I know," Mia grinned, "I can't wait to give Wish her presents so she feels even more special."

"I just wish we could stay here tonight," Alice sighed. "I'd love to wake up with Scout on Christmas morning."

Just as they'd finished their stables, a car pulled up and Alice's mum jumped out.

"Time to go home," she called across the yard.

"Do we have to?" Alice asked, half-joking. She'd jump at the chance of moving into Blackberry Farm to be near Scout all the time, but only if she could bring her mum and dad too.

"You'll be back here first thing tomorrow," Alice's mum laughed, "I don't think you're going to miss that much in the meantime, do you?"

After what had been going on in the last few weeks, the Pony Detectives weren't quite so sure. But now they knew that Mr Perryvale and his head lad were going to be investigated, they could sleep a bit easier, and finally look forward to Christmas Day.

ᘒ ᘒ ᘒ ᘒ

Mr Honeycott dropped the four friends off at the Abbey's main entrance a week later, on New Year's Eve. The girls squeaked with excitement as they waved goodbye to Rosie's dad, then walked up the main drive. The sky was bright blue, and cloudless, but it was still freezing. Alice felt herself shiver and linked arms with Rosie to keep warm.

The car park at the top of the drive was lined with huge, flashy horseboxes. Polo ponies, gleaming in the winter sun, were tied to them in rows, standing patiently. None were from Perryvale, Charlie was pleased to see.

Throngs of people, dressed up in glamorous winter clothes and looking really smart, were milling about and chatting. Mia was dressed in her finest riding gear, including her elegant furry hat, so she looked as immaculate as most of the other guests. The other three had made a real effort too, but they were already looking whipped by the wind, and within seconds of arriving, Rosie had spilled a drink down her front, staining her jacket.

There were so many people busily swirling around them, they couldn't find Mr Pyke. There was a brass band playing off to the right, on the edge of the woods, and the arena, with fairy lights wound all around the seats, had been turned into a grotto. Waiters slinked through the crowd, holding out trays of nibbles and glasses filled with hot punch. Rosie clocked where the waiters were coming out from, and planted herself nearby. The others dragged her away after the fifth piping hot sausage roll had disappeared into her mouth.

"What?" she said with a muffled voice. "Nick said to help ourselves to anything we want, didn't he? I'm just doing as I'm told...!"

The others giggled, then Charlie spotted

Mr Pyke and Archie and started waving madly in their direction.

Mr Pyke beckoned the girls over, and showed them into the commentator's box. They sank into the plush cushioned seats and picked up their programmes. Charlie flipped hers over, and immediately felt her breath catch in her throat. She nudged the others. There, on the back of the program, was a magnificent photo of Cracker, in full flight. The day had been dedicated to his memory.

The crowd were now taking their seats in the arena. The brass band reached a crescendo, then suddenly all was silent. The Winter Cup was about to begin.

"I can't believe *we* get to sit *here*!" Mia giggled, getting unusually giddy as the polo players from the first two teams began to stream in. The commentator introduced the riders and their ponies as they entered the arena. The ponies were glossy, their tails strapped up neatly to stop the players' sticks getting caught in them. Their manes were neatly hogged, so they could feel the pressure of reins on their necks to help them turn in the blink of an eye. The commentator counted the ponies for each team, announcing that they were just waiting for one more. The girls could see India, riding the finely built Frostie, and Billy riding a handsome chestnut. It was Estoni that hadn't yet appeared.

As the umpires rode in, the commentator ran through the names of the players and their ponies, telling the spectators good humoured facts about each and causing ripples of applause and laughter.

"Well, these seats are to say thank you," Mr Pyke said, smiling at the girls. "If it wasn't for you four, I don't even know if the Abbey Polo Club would still be open!"

Archie grinned at them too.

"And there's one polo pony," Mr Pyke continued, looking back to the arena, "who certainly wouldn't be here today…"

As the girls followed Mr Pyke's gaze, an electric current rippled through the gasping crowd. Estoni entered the arena at a slick canter, sitting on top of a plunging, fly-kicking bay.

The Pony Detectives gasped, hardly daring to believe their eyes as they watched the familiar polo pony power across the arena.

"Stormchaser...?" Mia gulped. Her heart leaped wildly. She didn't understand – just one week ago, she'd cradled Storm's head in her arms, certain that his fate was sealed. And now here he was, about to play in the Winter Cup! A hundred questions rushed into her head, but her throat tightened and the words wouldn't come out.

"But... How come..." Charlie stuttered, looking as stunned as the other three.

Mr Pyke smiled, broadly. "One thing nobody should underestimate," he said, nodding towards the bay, "is Stormchaser's toughness. He is made of granite, not flesh and bone. I can't think of another horse or pony who would have been able to shrug off the strong sedation the vet gave him and walk out of that ditch when the cattle grid was cut away. Not only that, he was able to bite the vet, kick Nick and charge at me only a few minutes later. The only one he didn't lash out at was Estoni!"

"Storm just walked away with bruising and scratches," Archie said, as the girls looked round at each other, amazed and relieved all at once. "He recovered from his injuries almost at once. He wasn't even lame for more than a day!"

"He's got you four to thank for that," Mr Pyke said earnestly. "Stopping him before he reached the cattle grid was genius. It saved his life, there's no doubt about that. Nick's getting rid of that death trap, too. It's first on his list of New Year's resolutions!"

The girls grinned at him as the two teams lined up facing each other on either side of the arena. Suddenly the ball was thrown in, between the players, signalling the start of the first chukka. The crowd erupted into a huge cheer. The match was off. The commentator's box was filled with squeals and cries as the ball flew between players in each short burst of play. The teams chased after the ball, leaning far out of their saddles without any apparent fear. The girls sat on the edges of their seats, thrilled by the fast paced and daring game in front of them. Stormchaser's number of chukkas was restricted because, as recovered as he was, Nick and Estoni didn't want to push him. But every time he was in the arena, Rosie noticed that no other horse stood a chance against him, as he shouldered them off their line, allowing Estoni to make a play for the ball. Rosie was bursting with pride that her little mare had been brave enough to try and block his path, *and* had very nearly succeeded.

India sparkled, riding the swift Frostie. As the Pony Detectives watched the chukkas, Charlie suddenly realised something. Every time another polo pony closed in on Frostie, Stormchaser was by his side, as quick as a flash. He would barge in, protecting the more timid Frostie, releasing the smaller horse from the scrimmage so he could fly up the arena.

"Have you noticed what's going on?" Charlie grinned, turning to the others. "It's like Stormchaser's looking out for Frostie, just like Cracker used to!"

"Oh, those three always looked out for each other," Archie said, joining in the conversation. "Stormchaser, Cracker and Frostie – or, Thunder and Misty, to use their real names – were all bred at the same yard in Argentina, and were trained together. Thunder and Misty came as freebies with Storm, because Mr Perryvale paid such a whopping price for him. When Nick used to school them together, Storm and Thunder would clear a path, so that Misty could fly clear of the opposition. Nick always knew that as a threesome, Storm, Thunder and Misty would win them polo matches. Only, Mr Perryvale never bothered to find that out. He was too busy rubbishing them because *he* couldn't stay in the saddle on any of them. But Nick won't separate Storm and Misty, not ever."

The girls exchanged an amazed look at Archie's revelation, just as Storm thundered down the length of the arena, closing in on the ball and scattering the rival team's ponies in his path. Without even looking up, Estoni tocked the ball towards India. Misty was already at full gallop, picking the ball up with ease, before India swung her stick under Misty's neck and sweetly tapped it into the goal.

The commentary boomed out beside them.

"And it's Stormchaser and the Silver Mist who team up once more to give the Abbey Polo Club a three goal advantage in their opening match!"

"Silver Mist?" Charlie asked, turning to Archie with a frown.

"That's Misty's full name," Archie explained as the crowd erupted into wild cheers. The girls' mouths dropped open, then they broke into wide grins, knowing what each other was thinking without having to say a word. As they high fived each other, tears misted their eyes. The awesome threesome may have been broken up, but at least they knew that Misty's future at the Abbey was guaranteed.

As the morning flew by, an endless stream of beautifully trained ponies poured into the arena, representing different teams in different chukkas. Some riders swapped their ponies mid-chukka, riding to the edge and hopping from one saddle straight into the next. But Stormchaser was the one horse that created a real buzz around the arena – for his intimidating presence and unflinching bravery in the arena, and his crazy antics on the way out of it. And it was Stormchaser who helped the Abbey team reach the final. He didn't play in the final match itself, because he'd done enough for one day and was clearly tiring.

Without him, the Abbey team couldn't quite keep up the momentum, and they lost 7-5 to the hugely powerful Angel Polo Team, but being runners up in their first showing in the Winter Cup was still a cause for huge celebration afterwards.

Estoni came up to the commentary box and gave each of the girls a hug, before dancing off to carry on the party with Storm. Then India, Nick and Billy brought a couple of the older polo ponies into the arena as Nick and his team demonstrated how to hold a stick, how to turn and control polo ponies, and some of the basic moves in competitive play. A big bunch of local riders from Greenfield's, the Pony Club and local livery yards stayed behind to watch, cheering as Nick invited the four Pony Detectives into the arena to be the first to have a try.

As the girls mounted, giggling at the strange

feeling of ponies that weren't their own, they looked around at the crowd of horsey people who had stayed behind. It wasn't long ago that everyone was threatening to boycott the Winter Cup, and Nick's dream of making polo accessible to everyone in the local area looked to be in tatters. But now, with the team at the Abbey completely cleared of any wrongdoing, the Pony Detectives felt nothing but thrilled about the future of the new polo club, and the small part they'd played in saving it from ruin before it had even had the chance to get going.

The excitement must have transmitted into their sticks. Under Nick's guidance, the girls got the hang of the basics quickly, and soon the ball was flying between them.

"Your turn, Rosie!"

As the ball scuttled along the sand towards her, Rosie imagined that she was riding Cracker. She pressed her pony forward into a canter, and without thinking, she swung her stick. She closed her eyes in embarrassment, expecting to have missed the ball. Instead there was a clear 'tock' as she hit it bang on. As applause and whoops erupted around the arena, Rosie's eyes flew open.

"Goal!" India cheered.

Rosie glanced skywards, and broke into a smile. "That one was for you, Cracker," she said, before riding back to the others.

"I'm impressed," Nick smiled at the Pony Detectives, after the girls finished their taster sessions and slid out of their saddles. "I think we'll have to make you honorary members at the club, especially after everything you've done."

"Ooh," Rosie said, brightening. "Does that mean we get free hot chocolate and cake from the café?"

The other three groaned, tapping Rosie with their sticks.

"If you can score goals like that," Nick grinned back, "you can have as many cakes as you want. And listen, we're thinking of starting up a Junior Abbey team pretty soon. Are you interested?"

The four girls looked at each other. The last few weeks had thrown the hardest of cases at them, and now they were ready for some fun.

The others nodded enthusiastically, but left the talking to Charlie.

"You bet we are! Thank you, Mr Webb!"

"But can we bring our own ponies?" Rosie asked, worrying about Dancer feeling left out.

"If your pony can block Stormchaser and live to tell the tale," India smiled, "she deserves a place on the Junior team, no question about it!"

The Pony Detectives all broke into huge grins. It was only New Year's Eve, but the next year already promised to be the best one the friends had ever had.

Turn over for some fantastic pony tips from the Pony Detectives and their pals!

India's Guide to Polo Equipment

Polo is great fun but also fast and furious! With sticks and balls flying everywhere, it's important to protect both your pony and yourself during games.

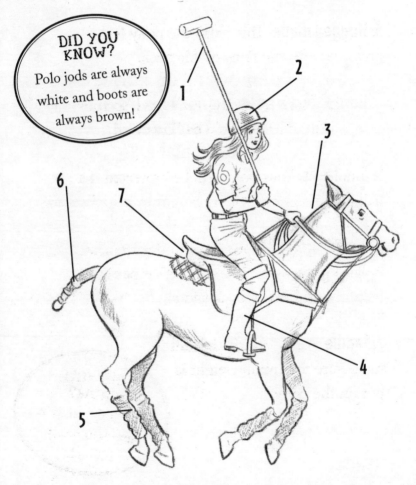

1. Stick These come in different lengths – the taller your pony, the longer your stick!

2. Helmet Some helmets have a guard on the front, in case the ball flies.

3. Hogged mane This helps the pony feel pressure from the reins on his neck.

4. Boots These are really, *really* hard, so your shin won't get bruised if a ball hits you!

5. Bandages Your pony will be protected if a ball hits him, or if he gets caught by a stick.

6. Taped-up tail Tape up your pony's tail, so it won't get tangled in a stick. It's especially helpful when doing back shots!

7. Saddle A polo saddle is built to make sure minimum weight is put on the pony.

DID YOU KNOW?
Polo balls can fly at speeds of nearly 100mph!

Plait Your Pony's Mane with Mia

Give your pony's mane a makeover with Mia's guide to perfect plaits.

1. Your pony's mane must be sparklingly clean! But, if it is too silky, the plaits will slip out. So, wash it the day before.

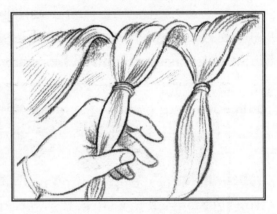

2. Divide the mane into small sections (about 3cm each) with rubber plaiting bands.

3. Dampen the section of mane you're about to plait.

DID YOU KNOW?
You need an even number of plaits in total. The forelock counts as one, so you should have an odd number of plaits along the neck.

3. Divide each section into three pieces and plait. Make sure the base is tight, so the plait doesn't go baggy when you roll it up! Finish with a plaiting band at the bottom.

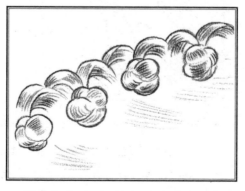

4. Fold the plait up under itself as many times as it allows, until you have a little bun. Put another band around each one.

How to Ride One Pony and Lead Another

Are the ponies friends? You don't want them nipping at each other, as it would make it hard to lead safely.

Are their heights similar? A smaller pony stretching his head up to a taller horse could hurt his back or neck.

India's tips

- ᘓ Practise first! Choose somewhere enclosed, like a sand school, and with someone responsible present.

- ᘓ Always keep the lead pony on your left, away from traffic.

- ᘓ Keep the led pony's head level with the ridden pony's withers.

- ᘓ Carry a short stick in your left hand, between the ponies.